I0683315

LES GRIS, THE SHADOW PEOPLE

The Illusionist Series
Book IV

by

Fran Heckrotte

2016

Les Gris, the Shadow People

Fourth in The Illusionist Series
Copyright © 2008 by Fran Heckrotte

All rights reserved.
ePub ISBN: 978-1-939950-20-8
Print ISBN: 978-1-939950-21-5
Mobi: 978-1-939950-10-9
First Published eBook: October 2008
First Print: January 2010
Publisher: Novel Ideas Publishing, LLC, Beaufort, SC. USA
Web Site: www.novelideaspublishing.com
Cover Design by Patty Henderson
Email: pattyghenderson@aol.com
Copy Editor: Cindy Burke
Website: www.cindyburke.com
Note: This edition has no major changes or additions to the story. The story has been revised for continuity purposes.

Acknowledgments

To all my beta readers (a very special group) who have taken this journey with me in telling the stories of my world of characters in The Illusionist series, thank you. You were instrumental in getting me to my destination without getting lost along the way. Lee McLean, Lori, Jae, Kimberly and Terry.

Pam, as always you've made sure the little things that could trip me up were caught in advance. You're a great safety net.

Patty Henderson, my cover artist. Great job again! I can't wait to see the next work of art you create.

Then there's Cindy Burke, my copyeditor. Small errors make big problems. You identified a lot of those that got by everyone else.

And as always, a special thanks to A. Lamarre, who encouraged me to write and inspired many of the stories I've written.

Oh, and Howie, of course. One day you may figure this one out. Thanks.

LES GRIS, THE SHADOW PEOPLE

CHAPTER 1

The Monster in the Closet

SOME CALLED IT a sixth sense or premonition. Randi knew differently, but rarely confided her secret. Most would think her crazy. The first time she had felt its presence she had been terrified. That was more than thirty years ago.

* * *

Hiding under the blanket, Randi was afraid to move, or even breathe. *Something* was in the closet. Something horrible. Something evil. There were no sounds, no movement, but that didn't prove anything. It was there. She could feel it and trembled, praying that her mom or dad would come to her rescue. A gentle click made her jump. Her heart thumped painfully. Soft footsteps approached and stopped at the side of the bed.

"Honey? Are you okay?" her mom whispered.

"Mommy?" Randi asked, her voice quaking.

"Yes, baby. What is it?"

"There's a monster in the closet. It's gonna get me."

"Oh honey, there's nothing there," her mother replied, pulling the blanket back to stare into frightened brown eyes. Gathering her daughter in her arms, she pressed Randi's head to her breast. "I'll show you."

"I'm scared."

"That's okay. You know I wouldn't let anything hurt you, don't you?"

Feeling the slight nod, her mother smiled and then gently pushed Randi away and back onto the bed. Walking to the closet, she opened the door and turned on the light.

"See! Nothing here, but your clothes and shoes."

"But I felt it, Mommy."

"Felt it?"

"You know! Like when you told Gram last week somethin' didn't feel right when we was walkin' in the park? Well, it don't feel right in here."

"I see. Well baby, sometimes our imagination plays tricks on us. How about I leave the bedroom door open tonight?" Glancing at the closet and then the door, Randi nodded.

"Good! If you feel something isn't right again, just yell and I'll be right here. How's that?" Leaning down, she kissed her daughter on the top of her soft brown hair and then gave her a hug. "Love you, pumpkin."

"I love you too, Mommy."

As she walked out of the room, Wanda smiled, remembering a time when she, too, believed there were monsters in the closet and under the bed. That was a long time ago. Unfortunately, her mother had died at childbirth and her grandmother had been indifferent to a child's fear. Wanda had sworn she would never let her own child suffer those same fears if she could help it.

As reassuring as her mother tried to sound, Randi was still afraid. There *was* something in the closet.

"I know you're there!" she whispered accusingly. She felt an invisible shiver and frowned. Maybe it wasn't so horrible after all. Horrible things weren't afraid of anything except mommies, daddies and baby Jesus.

"You're scared, aren't you?"

She felt another shiver and sat up.

"It's okay. I won' hurt you. You can stay in the closet," she offered bravely.

Feeling a sense of relief sweep over her, Randi giggled.

"You're just a big ba..."

The sound of footsteps interrupted her. When her mom stuck her head through the partially opened door, Randi waved.

"Time to go to sleep, sweetie."

"Okay."

"You still want me to leave the door cracked?"

"No, I was wrong, Mommy. There's no monster in there," Randi said, pointing to the closet. "The night light is enough."

"Super. Now, go to sleep. Tomorrow we're going shopping, remember?"

Nodding, Randi slid down under the sheets and closed her eyes.

"Night," she said, her eyes already feeling heavy.

"Night, baby."

Smiling, Wanda Brinley closed the door and went into the living room to watch television. Randi had always been a good child, easy-going and intelligent. She knew her daughter would believe her once she had proven the closet wasn't hiding monsters.

Back in the bedroom, Randi crushed her spare pillow against her chest and snuggled under her blanket.

"Night, monster," she teased. About to fall asleep, she felt a warm, tentative touch against her right ear and giggled. "Stop that!" she ordered good-naturedly, squiggling her head sideways and pressing it against her shoulder. "Go to sleep!"

* * *

For the next few years, Randi talked every night to the monster in the closet just before falling asleep. Although it never answered back, she could sense what it was feeling. Mostly it seemed afraid or sad. There were times, however, when she could tease it into a silent giggle or a happier mood. No matter what it was feeling, though, every night the monster would gently tickle her ear as she drifted off to sleep. The touch was reassuring.

When Randi was eleven, one night she decided that it was time for the monster to leave the closet. Her mom had just left the room after placing some folded underwear in the dresser drawer. Opening the closet door, Randi backed up and sat on the edge of the bed.

"Okay," she began. "You have to come out now." The monster shivered. Randi could feel the fear. "I'm not going to hurt you, but you have to come out. You can't stay in the closet all the time. Mom says we have to face our fears. That means you too." Nothing happened. "Come on," she coaxed.

Still nothing happened. Slapping her hands on the bed impatiently, Randi sniffed and then crossed her arms.

"If you don't come out, I won't be your friend anymore," she threatened. Randi suddenly felt an overwhelming sadness and relented. "Okay, I'll still be your friend."

Wondering how she could get the monster to come out, she thought about all those years it had hidden in the darkness.

"I've got it! I'll close my eyes. Then I won't see you come out." Again nothing. She walked to the half-open door and peered inside of the closet. "Phooey! You're just being stubborn."

Turning her back to the opening, she marched to the bed and threw herself on top, face down. After a few minutes, she felt her left ear being tickled. Randi decided to stay on her stomach for a little while longer. Obviously, the monster didn't want to be seen yet.

"You're supposed to be my friend. Mom says friends trust each other."

The monster shifted nervously.

"Well, I'm tired so I'm going to turn over now. You can sleep with me if you want. I won't hurt you and mom says I don't snore. I'd hate to snore, you know. Aunt Mary snores awfully loud and it keeps me awake when she visits."

When she turned over, Randi saw only darkness. Sighing, she pulled back the sheet and blanket, and crawled underneath.

"Night," she mumbled.

A slight tickling on her left ear couldn't lift her depression. Falling asleep, she felt the monster's sadness. Randi swore she'd figure a way to entice it out of its hideaway. Just not tonight.

In time she did, but not in the way she imagined or hoped for. For months, she tried to convince the monster to show itself. Then came a night when she was sure she had achieved her goal, only to discover it was no longer in her closet.

Randi was sad. She had tried and failed, or so she thought. It took a while before she realized it had become a part of her. A voice began to whisper in her head, warning her of impending danger. Soon the three of them grew comfortable with each other. *Three?* Somewhere, inside her, another *monster* waited patiently, biding its time for the right moment to appear.

CHAPTER 2

Randi, Lighthra and the Monster

THEY WERE INDIVIDUALS in spirit but the two of them shared the same body, and in so doing accepted that one of them would have to be dominant. The survival of both depended on the need to co-exist peacefully.

Lighthra loved her life-partner, Randi, more than anything or anyone. She and the human child were bonded.

The night the *monster* first appeared in the closet, Lighthra knew exactly what it was — a lost Shadow, *Les Gris* like herself, but not as fortunate. She could feel its pain and wanted desperately to help her kin.

At first, Randi had been afraid, but that soon disappeared. Although Lighthra couldn't communicate directly with her life-partner, she was able to calm the child's fears because of their close connection. Only then did Lighthra contact the lost Shadow.

You are Raylena. What happened? Lighthra asked. *Les Gris* could always recognize each other even if they had never met before. They never questioned how. It was simply a mystery that was accepted. *Where is your life-partner?*

Dead!

You should have passed beyond, then. Why didn't you? Lighthra asked. *Les Gris* weren't supposed to exist after their life-partner died.

I was afraid. It was waiting for me just as my human died. The Shadow's fear was almost contagious. Lighthra felt cold.

It?

The demon. I could feel it just beyond the periphery, lurking. It wanted me.

Then it's true. The Shadow Demon is real! Terrified that it could hear them, *Les Gris* seldom spoke of the creature. Few wanted to draw attention to themselves.

Yes, and if I had passed with my life-partner, it would have captured me.

How did you manage to avoid the passing?

I waited! the Shadow said.

Waited? I don't understand.

When my life-partner passed beyond, I hid deep in her lifeless mind, not daring to even think. It was horrible. There was nothing of her essence to sustain me.

Lighthra shivered. She couldn't imagine staying with Randi's body beyond life. Death, or whatever lay beyond, would be welcomed at that point. For Raylena to make such a decision was proof enough of her fear and desperation to avoid the legendary Shadow Demon. *Les Gris* feared many things, but nothing as much as the "stealer of shadows."

How long did you have to wait?

An eternity...at least it felt that way. Probably minutes. I felt it hunting for me, but it seemed reluctant to enter the mind of the dead. It too must have feared the nothingness left behind. I barely managed to escape from my life-partner once the Shadow Demon left. It was like dragging myself through

7

the darkest night with no light to guide me. There was nothing for me to grab onto.

Lighthra understood what Raylena meant. Darkness was the worst possible time for Shadows. Their nebulous shapes became lost in the blackness, making it impossible for them to reach out and touch anything. *Les Gris* were dependent on their life-partner during those periods to sustain them. In return, they protected their life-partner by warning them of the dangers lurking in the darkness. Fear of the night wasn't because of overactive imaginations. It was necessary to the survival of both mortal and *Les Gris.*

How did you end up here?

I don't know. I moved from place to place. The demon kept hunting for me. Somehow, it knew I was still around. One night, during a full moon, I slipped in here through the open window and into the closet. I hated not having light but it felt warm and safe. The demon prowled outside, but for some reason, wasn't able to enter this room.

Well, you can't hide in here forever. You're not even supposed to be able to exist this long without your life-partner's essence.

I know. I'm growing weaker, but I would sooner pass into nothingness than let the demon catch me.

Lighthra had to agree. She would make the same choice if she were in Raylena's situation.

Stay then. I'll try to let Randi know you're not a threat. Maybe we can think of something to help you out.

Thank you.

* * *

Lighthra eventually did come up with a solution. Two years later, during a blood moon eclipse, she invited Raylena to join her and share Randi's body.

Even if it were possible, your life-partner hasn't given her permission.

Tonight it's possible but you must hurry. Randi won't mind. She's very kind.

Won't this unbalance both of you?

You and I will keep all of us in balance. We'll need to be careful, though. Our duties must be divided equally, and we'll have to discuss everything we don't agree on. Randi is still a child. Her mind and her essence must never be put in jeopardy. You must leave if we start to unbalance.

And if we can't agree on something?

Then I must have the final word. After all, she was my life-partner first.

Raylena knew Lighthra was right. Merging was her only hope, and Lighthra's offer to share Randi was more than generous. How could she not agree?

You are as kind as Randi. Thank you.

It will be fun having you with us! Now, when the eclipse begins, reach out and grab onto our essence. Look for the faint strand of light between the blue and the green. It's difficult to see but not impossible. Only that one will guide you to our core. Choose wisely.

And if I grab the wrong one?

You will be lost forever. Hold tight to the strand or the waning light will rip you from us. The pull of darkness is strong. I'll help you as much as possible but the bulk of the strength must come from you. Randi and I will look for the demon during the merging. If you make it through the full eclipse, then the new birth of the moon will replenish you and we'll become one.

9

And if I fail? Will Randi be harmed? She is very young, and not even aware of my existence.

She's aware...just not on a conscious level. My life-partner has a good heart and a strong will. That's all we'll need from her for now. There can be no failure. We may both be lost and the demon will gain two more Shadows, Lighthra warned.

Why are you taking such a risk?

We are Les Gris, the Shadow People. *We are one in spirit. Soon we'll be one in life.*

And they were. Although the transition was painful, they were surprised when the Shadow Demon failed to appear. Little did they know that It was busy elsewhere gathering as many Shadows as it could. One small *Les Gris* wasn't worth the hundreds it could harvest in a few hours.

CHAPTER 3

The Predator

HE WAS A PREDATOR. One of the worst kind. A coward hiding in the darkness waiting for the right victim to pass by. Ironically, he was aware of his failings but could do nothing to change them. The obsession started when he was fourteen. At first he thought it was only puberty, hormones kicking in.

The erections were an embarrassment, but nothing like the humiliation he felt when his friends continually teased him about them. Just the sight of an attractive girl or woman aroused him, making his groin ache.

It was impossible to ignore — and quite noticeable — considering he was very well endowed, much to the envy of his classmates. Perhaps that was why they never failed to razz him whenever his jeans bulged, causing him to unconsciously rub himself. With envy came cruelty.

Tonight, he was desperate. For years he had managed to control the urges, but now it was growing more difficult. He wanted a woman...any woman. This was the third night he had waited in the alley for one to walk by, hoping to catch her unaware.

Several had come close...so close, but then, at the last moment, they suddenly stopped and crossed the street or

11

turned back in the direction they had come from. Always, though...always, they peered into the darkness, looking directly at the spot where he was hiding. He knew they knew he was there, and his need grew, as well as his rage. It was as if someone or something had warned them of his intentions.

* * *

Watching this woman walking slowly toward him gave him hope, even though she seemed to stare unblinkingly in his direction. Something about her intensity made him shiver. Shaking his head nervously, he decided it was merely an illusion created by the hunger.

You're a fool, the voice whispered.

"Shut up!" the man replied angrily. "Just leave me alone!"

I'm part of you. I'll never leave you alone, and you'll never kill or harm a human as long as I exist.

The man tried in vain to ignore the whispers. Once, there was a time when he thought he could have any woman he wanted if he was patient enough. To his frustration, he discovered differently. He would stalk his chosen subject, learn her habits and wait for the right moment. That moment never came. The women sensed he was on the prowl or lurking in the darkness. He knew it because of the voice in his head.

"Who are you?" he demanded for the hundredth time. "Why are you torturing me like this?"

Torturing you? You accuse me of torture? You're a bigger fool than even I imagined. I'll tell you what real torture is! It's being forced to live with someone you despise. Day after day, night after night, there's no relief from the miserable existence of this insufferable attachment we share. You're a sickness of the worst kind, and I can do nothing to rid myself of you. That

12

is torture. I can only hope that somehow I'll bring about your death soon. Only then will I be free.

The man cringed from the sheer hatred in the voice. Its wrath felt like a hot knife slicing through his brain. Desperate to shut it out, he cupped his hands over his ears and closed his eyes. After several minutes of silence, he opened them and found himself staring at a woman standing only a few feet away. Startled, he lowered his hands and stepped back, hoping the darkness would conceal him. The voice had left him too unsettled to think.

"Are you sure he's there?" the woman asked.

Frowning, the man glanced around to see whom she was talking to, but saw no one. Thinking she must be talking to someone out of his view, he held his breath and waited.

CHAPTER 4

Belle

"**I** KNOW YOU'RE IN THERE," Belle said, addressing the man hiding in the alley. "You might as well show yourself." When she received no answer, she cocked her head slightly as if listening for something more than a voice. "I can help you. You suffer greatly." Still no answer. "Tell him to come out," she continued. "Hiding in there isn't going to accomplish anything for either of you."

"How...how," the man stammered.

She talks to me, the voice hissed to his human. *I am the one who suffers the most, not you.*

Fear surged through his body like an electrical shock.

Who is she? What does she want?

You, you fool! She wants to save you! To save us!

Sa...save me? From what?

From yourself! From me!

"Listen to him," the woman advised, interrupting the mental battle between the man and the voice. "He'll destroy you if you don't let me help."

Realizing it was useless trying to stay hidden, the man eased away from the wall and stepped into the dimly lit area to stand in front of the strange young woman. She was several inches shorter than him and fat. He wondered why he had even considered attacking her. Making eye contact, he frowned at the vacant stare she gave him.

"You're blind!"

When she laughed, he thought she was even crazier than he.

"I see well enough," she replied. "How else would I know you were hiding in there? What's your name?"

"Sa...Sammy."

Without saying another word, she turned and walked away. Sammy stood watching, confused.

Follow her, stupid! There may be hope for us yet!

Grumbling to himself, Sammy did as he was ordered, feeling he had little choice.

* * *

The woman moved slowly down the street toward a twenty-four-hour restaurant several blocks away. Although her gait was slow and precise, no one would have suspected she was blind. Then again, it was only when she was on her nightly crusades that she left her dark glasses and cane at home.

Entering the restaurant, Belle moved to a booth close to the restrooms. It was somewhat secluded, giving her the privacy she needed. Reluctantly the man followed, but hesitated when she motioned him to sit.

"What's the matter? You can't be afraid of a blind woman. Only a few minutes ago you were more than willing to attack me," Belle growled and then laughed. Cowards were so predictable. "Well, either sit or leave, but don't stand there like an idiot." Nervously, the man sat down. "That's better. Now, tell me about the voice."

"Voice?" he stammered, glancing around to see if anyone was near enough to hear. "What voice?"

"Don't be an ass. You know damned well what voice. The one in your head."

"I...uh...it..."

"Never mind. I'll tell you about it. It taunts you, doesn't it? Berates you! You have *urges* and it won't let you fulfill them. It must be frustrating." It was a simple statement that held no empathy.

Sammy didn't know what to say. This woman seemed to know more about him than he did himself, and frustration was putting it mildly.

Poor Sammy, the voice hissed. *Not only do I frustrate you but now this blind woman knows all about us.*

The mocking laughter grated on his nerves, making him want to strike out at the woman.

"I wouldn't," she warned, staring blindly but unerringly into his eyes.

Flinching, Sammy looked away. Something about the unblinking stare unnerved him. He felt vulnerable and was frightened. She seemed to know his thoughts.

"What do you want?" he whispered, his voice trembling.

"That depends on you. What do you want?"

"I don't understand."

"Sure you do. Do you want to go on like you are or do you want the voice to go away?"

"Of course I want it to go away. It's driving me nuts."

"I don't know about that. I'd say it's saving your life," Belle replied. She stopped as the waitress walked up, placed two glasses of water on the table and got ready to take their orders.

"Hey Ms. Belle, how you doin' tonight?" Sassy asked, giving the man a curious glance.

16

"Fine, Sassy. I'll have the usual. Sammy here would like a cheeseburger and fries."

"Comin' right up."

"How'd you know my name and that I like cheeseburgers?"

"Everyone likes cheeseburgers. It was a safe bet," she replied, ignoring his other question. "Now, about the voice. When did you first hear it?"

Leaning back in the booth, Sammy thought about the question and the strange young woman sitting across from him. She wasn't the least bit good-looking. Mousy brown hair hung in curls down to her shoulders. Short bangs made her plump face look even fuller. Estimating her height at around 5'4, he guessed she was about thirty pounds overweight. Shaking his head, he wondered why he had even considered her as a potential target.

Because you're an ass like she said. You'd fuck a dog if you could!

"Go away!" Sammy muttered.

Again the laughter mocked him.

"It's annoying isn't it!" Belle said.

"What do you know about it?" he demanded angrily.

"Oh, I know a lot. I know how it mocks you. The annoying laughter. I'm surprised you've managed to keep what little sanity you have left." Sammy's eyes narrowed slightly. Was she being sarcastic or serious? "Sammy, Sammy, you need to lighten up. Oh well, maybe in time."

The appearance of the waitress interrupted their conversation.

"Here you go, Ms. Belle, BLT, extra bacon and no mayonnaise — and a cheeseburger and fries. Do you need anything else?"

"No thanks, Sassy. This is great."

Walking away, Sassy gave the man another curious glance and shook her head. Ms. Belle had been coming to the diner on a regular basis for almost three years. Normally, she was alone but occasionally someone was with her. They always looked so — *desperate,* Sassy thought. At least, at first. By the time Belle and her guests left, they seemed *different* — as if relieved of a burden.

Sammy's eyes followed the waitress as she walked away.

Not bad, he thought, feeling the urge start to rise. A light slap on the cheek startled him. He turned to glare at the woman sitting across from him

"What the hell was that for?"

"She's not for you."

Leaning forward, he squinted into Belle's eyes, looking for...

For what?

"Are you sure you can't see?"

Ignoring the question, Belle took a bite of her sandwich and chewed slowly, relishing the flavor of the bacon and tomatoes. Sighing in frustration, Sammy picked up his burger and chomped angrily down on it.

Shit! Woman's either psychic or nuts!

She's neither, the voice replied, *but don't be fooled by her blindness. There's more to her than you could ever contend with.*

I have no interest in her. She's freakin' damned weird.

Maybe, but she's the only hope we have at being normal.

Well, if being normal means getting rid of you, then I'll do whatever she wants.

When there was no response, Sammy felt uneasy. The voice had been with him for a long time. As much as he resented its interference in satisfying his urges, he realized it was the only thing that had kept him from becoming the monster he knew he would be without it.

Are you there? he asked tentatively.

I'm always here! I've told you I will never leave you. If I could, I would have a long time ago. We are the same, you and I. Only I'm not the monster you are. I was just unlucky enough to be your life-partner.

Life-partner? What the hell is that?

That, as you say, is me...or you, depending on who's talking. We were joined at your birth, unfortunately, for me, that is. Now I'm stuck with you and unless you let this human and her Les Gris help you — help us — I'll make your life a living hell beyond your wildest imagination, just as you've made mine.

What's so special about her?

Her life-partner. Their union is rare — the perfect merging of two unique entities. Between them, they may be able to make us whole.

Sammy wasn't sure what to think. Although he had grown used to being harassed by the inner voice, having a rational, civil conversation with it was a little disconcerting. On the other hand, it was a relief.

"Are you finished?" Belle asked, swallowing the last bite of her sandwich.

Blinking, Sammy realized he had only taken one bite of his own, but didn't feel hungry. Tossing it on the plate, he wiped his hands on his pant legs.

"I'm not hungry," he grumbled.

"I wasn't talking about your food. Do you want help? If not, say so. I don't want to waste any more time. There are others who need our help."

Sammy nodded his head slowly. What choice did he have? If she could help him, maybe one day he'd be able to find...looking longingly at Sassy, he swallowed.

Someone? A soft, unfamiliar whisper asked. Unconsciously, he nodded.

Then open your mind and let me in, it whispered.

The healing began. It would take time to change a lifetime of cravings and overcome his natural tendencies. Belle would have to enlist the aid of The Society to balance him and his life-partner, but for now she could stabilize him temporarily.

CHAPTER 5

Belle and Lunara

IT WASN'T SUPPOSED to happen. At least that was what the doctors had told her. Minor head injuries rarely caused blindness. Sure, it had hurt when she fell, striking her head on the edge of her best friend's bed, but she hadn't even lost consciousness. A golf ball sized bump was the only evidence of her reckless antics and youthful exuberance.

The doctor at the emergency room assured her parents that after a few days of rest, their daughter would be back to normal. And she was — for a while. Even when she noticed her vision changing, the ophthalmologist said it wasn't unusual for a teenager to need glasses. Later, he realized her visual loss was progressing too rapidly to be an ordinary eye disorder. After running additional tests, he diagnosed her with bilateral optic nerve atrophy. Belle's entire world collapsed. The future of a sixteen year old girl should be bright. Hers would be dark and lonely, or so she thought.

* * *

It had taken a long time for Belle to accept that she would never see again. Sometimes she wished she had died instead of facing a world of darkness. Having to depend on others was humiliating enough. The thought of not even being able to enjoy a good book or party with friends or go for quiet walks without the aid of someone else had been too much for the sixteen year old. Withdrawing into herself, she distanced herself from everyone — until the whispers began.

Are you going to keep feeling sorry for yourself?

Belle rolled over on her side, thinking she was dreaming.

I'm not a dream. You can try to ignore me but it won't do any good. I've worked too hard to make you hear me.

Turning on her other side, Belle punched the pillow several times before again settling down.

"Go away," she grumbled, thinking someone was playing a trick on her.

I can't. You won't let me.

"That's ridiculous. I didn't tell you to come in here. Now go away."

It's not possible. I'm a part of you.

Sitting up, Belle moved her head, searching for the source of the voice.

"Where are you? Who let you in my room?"

You let me in. Now, are you ready to start living again or do you want to spend your life hiding in here and sulking?

"I'm not hiding or sulking, and I'm perfectly fine."

Sure you are! You only leave this room to eat and use the bathroom. Your family and friends may have given up on you, but I won't. I can't.

"Okay, I'm getting pissed. Someone put you up to this, didn't they? Well I'm not that stupid, so just stop it and get out!"

The laughter was infuriating. It mocked her.

No, you're not stupid, so quit acting like it — and stop feeling sorry for yourself. It's time to take your life back.

It was Belle's turn to laugh. The bitterness behind it almost choked her.

"Yeah, right! Well, perhaps no one's told you I'm blind, so just how am I supposed to do that?"

You have me. I'll help you.

"You? Are you going to be my seeing-eye dog? Lead me by the hand everywhere? Pretend to be my eyes?"

Yes! That's exactly what I will be. Your eyes.

It wasn't the answer Belle expected, and she didn't know how to respond.

"Who are you?"

You know who I am, Belle. There was once a time when we played together, but that was long ago.

"When? I don't remember you."

Again the laughter, only this time it was gentler.

Like I said, it was a long time ago. You were just a child and far more believing than you are today.

Belle frowned, trying to remember her younger years, and then her sightless eyes opened wide as visions of the past flashed before her like a movie playing in reverse.

* * *

Tamara O'Reilly shook her head as she put the covered dish in the refrigerator. She was at her wit's end. Walking into the living room, she plopped down on the couch next to her husband, causing him to knock his teeth on the beer bottle he had just placed against his lips.

"Sorry," she muttered and patted his cheek affectionately.

Gripping his front tooth with his fingers, he checked it to see if it had damaged the cap protecting the stub.

"Thas okay," he replied, releasing the tooth. "She's still being difficult, I take it."

"Yeah. I'm not sure what to do anymore. If she doesn't start school next week, the board says they'll have to take some type of action. I wish we could afford a tutor."

"I know, but we're barely making ends meet as it is. I suppose I could ask Grams for a loan," he offered hesitantly. He knew what that would entail. His grandmother would gladly give him what he needed. Unfortunately, she always exacted a heavy price from anyone in her debt. Harvey felt like it was selling his soul. She would expect him to be at her beck and call from then on.

"Not after seeing what Sally went through," Tamara growled. "Grams can keep her damn money. We'll figure something..."

Before she could finish, the sound of a door slamming startled them. Glancing toward the stairs, Tamara and Harvey were surprised to see their daughter standing at the head of the steps.

"Are you alright, honey?" Tamara called out, jumping to her feet.

"Yes, mother," Belle replied, sounding exasperated.

Tamara looked at Harvey nervously. It was rare their daughter left her room.

"I want to go to Chisolm Park," Belle announced.

"Umm, it's almost six o'clock. It'll be dark in about an hour or so."

"Really, mother. What difference does that make to me?"

Realizing the stupidity of her comment, Tamara's eyes welled up with tears.

"What your mom means, honey, is that the park may not be safe," Harvey said, wanting to diffuse the situation. "Tomorrow's Saturday. Can we go then?"

"No, I want to go now. I have to go now."

The desperation in Belle's voice was enough to sway Tamara. Harvey, however, still wasn't convinced of the necessity of risking his family's safety in an area that had become somewhat questionable as far as security. Seeing his hesitation, his wife touched his arm gently.

"Please," she mouthed.

Giving up, he nodded.

"Okay, get your jackets and we'll go, but we're not staying once the sun sets."

Thirty minutes later, Tamara and Harvey watched their daughter walk toward the merry-go-round.

"It's like she can see," Harvey whispered, not wanting to be overheard.

"She spent a lot of time here when she was a kid. I guess she can remember a lot about it."

"I guess. It still seems freaky, though."

"I know."

Moving to sit on a bench, they glanced around to see who else was at the park. Standing near a street light, a cop was talking into his shoulder mic. An older couple was moving toward their car, the man leaning heavily on his cane while the woman gripped his arm. It was obvious she was guiding him.

"That's us in thirty years," Harvey said and smiled.

"Oh, I think we'll have a few more years than that before we reach that stage," Tamara said, sliding closer to her husband.

"I can only hope. Why do you think Belle wanted to come here now? I mean, this is the first time she's shown an interest in doing anything."

"I don't know, sweetie. This was one of her favorite spots. Maybe she's just trying to recapture those good moments."

"I guess."

They both continued watching Belle, remembering fondly the times their daughter ran up and down the park, chasing her invisible friend.

"Do you remember..." Harvey started to ask but couldn't think of the friend's name.

"Looney!" Tamara supplied and then laughed. "How could I forget? Those two were inseparable."

"I should hope so. After all, she was imaginary."

"Well, imaginary or not, Belle loved her. That's all that mattered then."

Harvey nodded. Before he could say anything else, he saw his daughter grab the handle of the merry-go-round and give it a spin. Then she turned and started walking toward them.

"We can go now," Belle called out. "I'm hungry. Can we get a Chicken-Taco wrap?"

Surprised, neither parent answered for several seconds. Finally, Tamara stuttered a weak "yes" and grabbed her husband's hand squeezing it. Something miraculous had happened, but neither of them dared to question what or how.

* * *

That had been eighteen years ago. Since then, Belle had graduated from college, earning a degree in literature with a minor in paranormal psychology. When an assistant professorship job opened up at her alma mater, a friend encouraged her to apply. With Lunara's help, the interview went smoothly and she was quickly hired. Now, at thirty-four, she had full tenure as a professor of literature. Although the pay wasn't great, it gave her enough for a comfortable life and the time to pursue a second career.

You call this a career? Lunara asked, laughing softly.

26

"Well, it is...sort of. Granted it's not exactly a textbook job, but at least I know I've helped a few people and their life-partners. I wish I had been able to save all of them."

Me too, but some humans are too far gone. It's bad enough when the two are out of sync but if the Shadow is lost or detached, only a blood moon can re-establish the connection. There are so many unbalanced life-partners and so few of us to help them. Tonight we're lucky. This human's life-partner has been able to control the man's urges up till now. I doubt if he could have lasted much longer, though.

Belle nodded as she listened to the sound of steps several feet behind her. Although she couldn't hear his Shadow's thoughts, Lunara could.

They are badly out of sync. I'm not sure we can resolve it entirely.

"We have to try. Even a partial victory may be enough to stop him from hurting someone. You said he was a predator. To fail with him isn't an option. Others will be harmed. I'm surprised he hasn't hurt anyone already."

Luscian wouldn't permit it!

"Luscian?"

His life-partner. He has been warning the other Les Gris whenever he could. They made sure their humans avoided him.

"Is Luscian stable?"

He's damaged but not irreparably so. If we can re-sync them, it should be enough to minimize the man's urges to a controllable level.

Belle chuckled softly.

"You always say *we* as if I really have much to do with that. You're the one who takes the risks. It can't be easy prying into a stranger's mind, searching for the causes of the imbalances. I don't think I could stand being that *intimate* with human neurosis and psychosis...and the phobias...well, they're..." Belle let the sentence drop, remembering her own fear as a child. How ironic that she had suffered achluophobia, fear of the dark, and now her entire world was exactly that most of the time.

There were moments, however, when she could share Lunara's vision of the world. The first occurred during solar eclipses when light rays from the sun were temporarily blocked. Normally a world in darkness weakened the Shadows' vision but the ionization of the atmosphere and refractive rays of the sun created anomalies that enhanced the light waves, fracturing them into kaleidoscopic colors. This was what Belle would see through the eyes and mind of Lunara.

During those moments their energies temporarily fused, providing each with an almost orgasmic pleasure. It was only when they were suddenly ripped apart by the waning eclipse, and resumed their normal existence, that both understood the pain and anguish of the detached or out of sync human and Shadow.

More often than the eclipse, though, was when Rainbow popped in to chat with Lunara. Highly animated, she always made seeing an interesting experience. Then again, what did one expect from a Boreal? Elementals, especially Boreal, were very light-hearted.

CHAPTER 6

The Invisible Friend

HIS FAMILY HAD ALWAYS thought he was a little crazy, but had attributed it to his premature birth. The doctors had warned them there were often complications from a poorly developed respiratory system. As a toddler, he seemed withdrawn and fearful. Later he complained about a ghost hiding under his bed. No matter how much they tried to assure him it was only his imagination, he refused to believe them. The voice proved him right.

Thomas would never forget the night it first appeared. His mom had just tucked him into bed and kissed him goodnight. She left the room, turning the light off behind her. Closing his eyes, Thomas wrapped his arms around Carlton the bear and smiled.

"Thomas", a voice whispered in the dark.

Opening his eyes, he looked around the room, expecting to see his mom. When he didn't see her, he frowned.

"Mom?"

"Thomas," the voice said again.

29

Sliding deeper into the sheets, he peeked over the edge. A small nightlight lit the room but there was nothing unusual to be seen.

"Don't be afraid, Thomas. I'm your friend, your magical friend." The voice was soft and reassuring.

"Oh!"

"You don't remember me?"

"Ummm, nooo," Thomas replied hesitantly.

"That saddens me. We used to play together when you were younger. Remember when you would make little animal shadows on the walls with your hands before your mother turned out the lights?"

"Uh huh."

"That was me!"

"You was the rabbit?"

"Yes, I was the rabbit and the bird and the dog."

"Mom says you was just shadows. It was a game."

"That's because your mom doesn't know about me. She can't hear me like you can."

"Oh!"

"You see, I'm *your* friend, not hers. Only you can hear me."

"Wow!" Thomas looked around for signs of the shadow animals he had made in the past. There was nothing. "How come I don' see you now? Where are you?"

"There's not enough light, but I'm right here."

"I want to see you," Thomas said, sitting up in his bed.

"Not tonight, Thomas. Your mom has turned out the light."

"I want to see you!" Thomas cried out.

"If you yell like that your mom will come and then I will have to go. Do you want that?"

"Nooo, but I want to see you now."

"You will have to be patient. If you do as I say, you can see me for a little while tomorrow."

"Promise?"

"Oh yes, I promise. We're going to spend a lot of time together, Thomas...a lot of time."

"Okay. I wait cuz you promised."

"Good! Now go to sleep."

Nodding his head, Thomas slid beneath the blanket and closed his eyes.

"That's good...very good", the voice whispered and then laughed softly.

The next night Thomas waited anxiously for his friend to appear. His mother hadn't come in to turn off the light yet, so he walked around the room peeking in the closet and under the bed.

"Where are you?" he asked hesitantly.

"I'm here," the voice whispered.

"I don' see you!" Thomas yelled.

"Be quiet!" the voice ordered sternly. "If your mom comes in, I'll leave," it threatened.

As tears welled up in his eyes, Thomas plopped down on the floor and whimpered.

"I want to see you. You promised!"

"Yes, but only if you do as I say. Stop crying. I don't like crybabies."

Instantly the tears dried up.

"That's good. Now, stand up and close your eyes."

Thomas did as he was instructed.

"Turn around and look at the wall."

Doing as he was told, Thomas gasped when he saw the dark shadow before him.

"Is that you?" His voice trembled with childish awe as he stared wide eyed at the gray form.

At first the voice didn't answer. Moving forward, Thomas reached out to touch the shadow.

31

"You forgot about me," the voice accused, almost poutingly.

"I didn' mean to."

"You hurt my feelings."

"I'm sorry," Thomas replied, shuffling his right foot nervously. "I was born bad mom says. Maybe thas why, huh?"

"Maybe," the voice conceded. "Only time will tell."

"Tell what? I don' understand."

"Never mind. I forgive you."

"Phew!" Thomas said, relieved that he had been forgiven. His mom had told him many times that forgiveness meant everything would be okay again. "Are we going to play now?"

"Yes, we can play."

Clapping his hands gleefully, he sat on the floor and listened while the voice instructed him on how to make shadow figures. Occasionally, his animals would move differently from the way his hands moved. Laughing, he would try to control the shadow.

When his mom walked in, he jumped up and looked at her, a big smile on his face.

"What are you doing?" she asked.

"Playin' with my friend."

"Your friend?"

"Yeah, mom, look!" he yelled enthusiastically. Turning, he made a shadow rabbit and laughed as he made its ears wiggle.

"Oh, I see! Well, it's time to go to bed so say good night to your friend."

"Okay! Night!" Thomas said, waving at the shadow on the wall.

Shaking her head, his mother waited patiently as he climbed into bed and under the sheets. Her son tried his best to be good but often lost his temper, and that led to tantrums. She prayed every night that he would grow out of them. It was moments like these that gave her hope.

"Did you say your prayers?"

"Oh, I forgot!"

Bowing his head, Thomas whispered a quick prayer and then looked up expectantly. He loved his mom but there were times when he imagined doing awful things to her, especially when she was mean to him.

"Good boy," his mom praised. Leaning down, she kissed him on the top of the head and then tucked the sheets around his shoulders.

"Sleep well. I love you."

"I love you too, mom."

After she left, Thomas looked at the far wall for signs of the shadow. The darkness made it impossible to see anything.

"You there?"

"I'm here, Thomas,"

"You didn' say night."

"I know. I was waiting for you to finish your prayer."

"Oh, yeah. I always say my prayer at night. Mom says I'll go to heaven when I die as long as I do it."

"Do you believe in heaven, Thomas?"

"Yes. Mom says thas where baby Jesus is. Daddy's with him."

"I see."

"Is your mom and dad in heaven?" Thomas asked, his eyes searching the darkened room for signs of the shadow. Other than the voice, there was nothing.

"I never had parents."

Thomas gasped.

"Everyone has a mom and dad."

"Why?"

"Because Mom said so."

"Ah. Well, parents don't always tell the truth, Thomas. Sometimes they say things to make their children feel better or behave."

"My mom don' lie!" Thomas cried, his lower lip sticking out stubbornly.

"Don't yell, Thomas. I said I don't like it when you yell."

The stern reprimand made the boy's eyes tear up.

"I sorry."

"That's better. As I was saying, sometimes parents want to protect their children or make them feel better so they tell stories. If you don't believe me, ask your mom when you wake up. Now, it's time you went to sleep. We'll play again tomorrow night."

"You mad at me?"

"No, but you mustn't question me when I tell you something. Tomorrow you will see that I always tell the truth. Good night, Thomas."

"Okay, night."

Closing his eyes, Thomas quickly fell asleep, relieved that his friend wasn't mad at him. The shadow patiently waited in the dark. His plans were progressing well.

* * *

For the next twenty years, Thomas' friend appeared every night in the bedroom, subtly manipulating the child and then the adult until eventually, it was able to control him. It would be years until Thomas discovered who his childhood companion really was and what his motives were.

CHAPTER 7

Angie, Sylvie, Soleil and Lumiere

THE LIGHT WAS Angie's life. It nourished her, warmed her and soothed her. Her world was bright and warm and beautiful, A kaleidoscope of colors constantly moving about in an endless dance...until the darkness crept in, obliterating the light. Were it not for her spouse, the darkness would have been unbearable. As if in response to her thoughts, a soft caress touched her skin. Her life-partner shivered with pleasure along with her.

"You are so beautiful," Angie whispered, leaning down to kiss the warm lips of the woman lying in quiet repose beneath the satin sheets.

"Apparently you're not wearing your contacts, again," her wife Sylvie teased. "Lucky me!"

"Lucky both of us then. In my blindness I see beauty. In yours you see the ordinary."

"Aren't you the philosopher tonight!" Sylvie taunted and then squeaked when she was abruptly poked in the ribs.

"You're awfully brave considering I have the advantage," Angie said.

"Well then, why is it taking you so long to use it?"

Sylvie's voice was soft and whispery. Her warm breath smelled of chocolate and mint, the after-effects of a peppermint patty she had been eating only minutes earlier.

Leaning down, Angie kissed her gently, trying not to touch her wife's injured shoulder. When Sylvie gasped, Angie pulled back and frowned.

"Did I hurt you? Are you in pain?"

"No and no. I'm fine, but there's no need to hurry."

"It's just been too long since we've made love. I'm hungry."

"Three days. I fell down those blasted steps just three days ago."

"That's an eternity," Angie said, "but I don't want to rush you. The doctor said you need to be careful for another couple of weeks."

"He said *careful*, Angie. He didn't say anything about celibacy. Besides, you've always wanted to be a top. Now's your chance. I promise not to resist too much." She smiled teasingly.

Both of Angie's eyebrows shot up. She gave Sylvie an exaggerated, haughty look.

"My, my, but you are asking for it, aren't you?"

Sylvie grinned again. "Do I have to ask?" She already knew the answer.

Pulling off her tee shirt and undies, Angie climbed over her lover and slipped under the sheets.

"Do you want the light off?" she asked.

"No. I like to watch you when we make love," Sylvie said. "I love how your eyes light up and how serious you sometimes look when you're concentrating on pleasing me. I want to see the sweat glistening on your shoulders and trickling between your breasts. Besides, it makes our Shadows happy."

Angie laughed.

"You and your Shadows. You've been talking about our Shadows for over sixteen years. I still can't believe you think they're alive."

Sylvie grinned.

"They are! Watch!"

Moving her arm slowly she watched her shadow as it mimicked her movements. Angie stared in amusement as the dark arm slid across the dimly lit wall and came in contact with her own shadow at the very moment Sylvie's hand caressed her left breast. When Angie shivered, Sylvie smiled.

"Now tell me your Shadow didn't enjoy mine's touch."

"When you do that, I'll tell you anything you want to hear," Angie gasped, her heart racing. The pulse in her neck beat furiously. She wondered if her shadow was feeling the same way and then mentally shook her head.

You'd believe Etheridge was straight if it got you laid! Angie's conscience never let her get away with anything, but if Sylvie wanted to believe in Shadows, that was okay.

They had been married for several years and, hopefully, would be for many more to come. Just the thought made her feel warm and loved. Leaning across her wife, she began to slowly explore the sensitive areas of Sylvie's body that she had discovered after years of experimentation.

Occasionally, though, she would glance at their shadows as they moved in sync with her and Sylvie and couldn't help but wonder — what if she was right? What if their shadows were alive? Did hers feel what she felt? Did they understand love and longing and joy? Angie hoped so and quickly forgot the thought as her tongue traced its way down her wife's warm body to the right thigh and then the knee. Puckering her lips, she sucked gently on the skin and then began moving up the inside of Sylvie's thigh toward the musky scent teasing her nostrils.

"You smell so good," She groaned.

Sylvie shifted her left leg slightly, opening herself to her lover's touch. Her leg quivered as if straining but both knew it was from anticipation. Angie knew her lover's body well. Her tongue flicked the moist skin and then teased the hairs that concealed what she sought.

As Sylvie arched upward to meet her, she felt a slight twinge in her left shoulder. Before she could react, a warm hand covered it and then disappeared beneath its surface. The pain quickly disappeared. Turning her head, she glanced at the two Shadows on the wall and smiled.

Thank you, she mouthed, then lost herself in Angie's adept lovemaking. The two Shadows smiled at each other and silently exchanged giggles.

If only Angie knew what Sylvie knows, one thought.

And where's the fun in that?, the other replied, embracing her Shadow lover intimately. They, too, became lost in their union. They were fortunate. Not only were their life-partners well suited to each other, but they had found their own energies pleasingly compatible. Although they could communicate with each other anytime they wanted, the moments when they could touch each other were precious. It wasn't often that lovers chose to display their intimacy in the light.

As Angie continued stroking Sylvie with her tongue, she could feel her wife's body responding. Moisture pooled between warm thighs. Legs trembled. Short gasps and soft groans told Angie that she was succeeding in her efforts to please her lover. Separating the thick lips with her tongue, she buried her face in the warmth and inhaled deeply.

I could die here, she thought and then mentally chuckled. *But I don't think Sylvie would be too happy.*

The Shadows stopped their own explorations and shook their heads.

Humans!

* * *

Satiated, Angie rolled over on her back and stared at the ceiling.

"Wow, that was intense!" she gasped, her voice husky.

As her heartbeat gradually slowed, she turned to stare at Sylvie and smiled. "You all right?"

"Oh, yeah! Just trying to catch my breath," Sylvie whispered. Reaching out, she gently stroked Angie's cheek and then let her eyes wander to the Shadow on the wall that was emulating her movements. Nodding her head in that direction, she turned Angie's head toward the gray shapes.

"They're happy, too."

Angie laughed.

"You are such a romantic. I think that's one of the things I love most about you. You see the good in everything."

"Well, someone has to. Can you imagine living with someone who sees only the bad in people? What an awful way to live," Sylvie replied, poking Angie in the ribs. "Thank goodness you're beginning to see the light. You were such a stick in the mud when I first met you."

"Stick in the mud! I'll have you know I've never been a stick in the mud, thank you very much," Angie said, fcigning indignation. She knew Sylvie was right but wasn't about to admit it.

"Okay, maybe not...but you sure were angry looking."

"So why'd you approach me?"

"I was curious and...I don't know...I got this sudden feeling that you were more lost than angry. It's hard to explain."

Angie frowned, remembering back to a time that she would have preferred to forget. Sylvie had asked if she could imagine living with someone who only saw the bad in people. She didn't need to imagine. Aunt Jenny was that person.

* * *

She had just turned sixteen when her mom died. That was putting it nicely. Suicide wasn't about dying. It was about destroying those you'd left behind who cared about you, and not giving a damn. At least that was how Angie felt at the time and she was angry...angry at being abandoned and angry at having to live with an aunt who continually reminded her of her mom's faults and selfishness.

She would never forget the day that changed the rest of her life. Aunt Jenny barged into her small bedroom at 7:30 in the morning, demanding that she get her lazy ass out of bed and get dressed.

Put on something nice, she had said. Her mom's attorney was coming over to discuss her estate.

"I hope your mother at least left enough money for me to cover her burial expenses. Twenty-three hundred dollars to cremate someone. What a ripoff! No one's worth that much money dead. And you!" Aunt Jenny spat, pointing an accusing finger at Angie. "Lord knows I don't make enough money to feed and clothe you.

"Colleen was always a selfish bitch. Getting knocked up by that man when she couldn't afford to raise a child. I told her to get an abortion but she wouldn't hear of it. Now she goes and kills herself and leaves me stuck with a lazy good-for-nothing."

Stomping out of the room, Jenny slammed the door behind her. Angie's eyes clouded with unshed tears but she forced them back. She would never allow her aunt to see her weakness.

Thirty minutes later, she reluctantly walked down the stairs and entered the living room. A tall, gray haired man was sitting in the worn, green recliner, shuffling through some papers. He and Jenny glanced up. Her aunt frowned.

"Jesus Christ, Angie. Do you always have to dress like a boy? I'd have thought Colleen would at least have trained you how to dress properly." Turning to the man, she shook her head in disgust. "Kids nowadays! It's no wonder the world's going to hell." She looked at her niece. "You just march right upstairs and put on a dress. I'll not have Mr. Pierce thinking I'm raising a tomboy — or worse, a dyke."

The man's eyes narrowed slightly. Henry Pierce had always detested Colleen's sister. She was a vindictive, ill-tempered shrew. Why his client had left her as her child's guardian was beyond him. He gazed at the sad girl with the short, dark spiky hair.

"She's just fine, Ms. Hampton. Now, I have another appointment at ten so we need to get this finalized. Please have a seat, Angie."

Doing as she was instructed, Angie leaned back in the chair and waited. She had met her mom's attorney twice before and liked him.

"I'm sorry for your loss, Angie. I know this is hard on you," Mr. Pierce said, sympathetically. "I've known your mom since she was a little girl." Coughing slightly, the attorney turned his attention to the paperwork in his hands.

"First, the good news is that there's enough money in the estate to pay for her funeral. She took out a small insurance policy a few years ago specifically for that. You should be receiving a check from the agency in a week or two."

"At least she did something right," Jenny said, relieved that she wasn't going to have to foot the bill.

"Please, Ms. Hampton," Mr. Pierce admonished.

Blushing at the obvious reprimand, Jenny clamped her jaws tight. Alienating her sister's attorney wasn't wise.

"Now where was I? Oh yes, the funeral. As I was saying, there's an insurance policy that will cover that. Also, she has a small trust account for you, Angie, with about ninety-eight thousand dollars in it. That should more than cover your care for the next two years with enough left over for college if that's what you want. Of course, at the moment, your aunt is in charge of the trust but when you turn eighteen, you'll be able to do with it whatever you want."

Angie sat in stunned silence. Two years was a long time, but she could handle it if she had something to look forward to. Surely, she'd have at least half of that left by the time she was eighteen.

"Ninety-eight thousand dollars!" Jenny exclaimed. "How'd Colleen save that much?"

"She was very frugal and made a few good investments. It was important to her that Angie have something if anything happened to her."

"Thank goodness for that, anyway. Not that ninety-eight thousand dollars goes very far nowadays. It'll barely cover the cost of feeding and clothing this child."

"Ms. Hampton, you do understand that this money can only be used on Angie's behalf?"

"Of course, of course."

Secretly, Jenny was already thinking of the things it would buy, and none of it had to do with her niece.

"Good! Well, all I need is your signature on a few documents. As executor of your sister's estate, you're responsible for making sure everything is taken care of according to Colleen's wishes. I'll require an expenditure sheet once a month. Make sure you account for all funds you withdraw from Angie's trust."

After getting her aunt to sign the papers, Mr. Pierce gathered his briefcase, hat and coat. Patting Angie on the shoulder, he left.

Turning to Angie, Jenny frowned.

"Don't go thinking I forgot about you and the way you're dressed. Just look at those jeans — faded with holes in the knees. You intentionally put those rags on to embarrass me. It's no wonder your mother did what she did. You get your —"

"Fuck you!" Angie screamed and stormed out the front door, slamming it loudly.

"You ungrateful brat!" Jenny yelled after her. "Don't think you'll get away with talking to me like that! I'll have you arrested and locked up!"

Angie didn't know whether she was angrier at her aunt's cruelty or her mom's betrayal for leaving her with the one person she had hated most of her life. Aunt Jenny had always been critical of Colleen and her daughter. Why, Angie neither knew nor cared.

* * *

"Earth to Angie, Earth to Angie," a voice whispered in her ear.

Turning her head slightly, Angie stared at its owner for a few seconds and then grinned sheepishly.

"Sorry, I was just remembering back to when we first met. I think you saved my life that day."

As much as Sylvie wanted to deny it, in her heart she suspected there was some truth in her lover's statement.

"It was a pretty rough time for you. I'm just glad the fates brought us together at that moment."

Angie rolled her eyes.

"First it's the Shadows, now it's the fates. Sixteen years together and you still haven't changed." She smiled at her wife affectionately.

"And I never will, so you might as well not get your hopes up. Besides, even if you don't believe me, I happen to know we were destined to be together."

Angie smiled.

43

"Now *that* I believe!"

Well, at least there's hope for your life-partner, Sylvie's *Les Gris* Lumiere said, nudging Soleil with her shadowy elbow.

Behave!

If a Shadow could roll her eyes, Lumiere would have done so.

You're just as bad as your human! She said.

Look who's talking. Now hush!

Because of their positions, neither Sylvia nor Angie could see the disgruntled Shadow crossing her arms.

Cupping Sylvie's chin in her hand, Angie rubbed her thumb gently back and forth over her cheek.

"I'm serious. The few months we were together made me realize I might have a chance at a future. That day was the start of my life."

"Mine, too. I couldn't believe it when your aunt called the police on you. She was such a bitch."

"Yeah, she knew I was going to stay over at your place. I left a note on the table telling her. It was just an excuse to get me out of the picture and her hands on my money after I accused her of stealing some of it."

"I know, but I never understood why she called my mom and told her those lies about us — not that I *wasn't* thinking about you that way. I mean, your kisses were driving me nuts."

"Aunt Jenny was a miserable person. If I hadn't hated her so much, I'd have felt sorry for her. I was glad when she died."

"Me too! I can't believe Mom actually thought sending me to a convent for six months would straighten me out. If she only knew what I learned there."

Sylvie and Angie laughed. Sister Charlene had given Sylvie quite an education.

"Yeah, I have to admit you learned a few skills that even I had never heard of."

"Well now, that's saying a lot."

Again they laughed. Angie had spent almost two years as a ward of the state because of her aunt. Jenny had called the police, claiming her niece ran away from home. Pretending concern, she had told the officers, and later the judge, that Angie might be suicidal like her mother. Jenny pleaded for them to help her beloved niece.

Being a minor, Angie stood no chance against the accusations and was sent to the state youth center for sixteen months for rehabilitation. During her incarceration, she discovered a whole new world of bad girls and how to be one herself. When she finally was released on her eighteenth birthday, she knew more about the female anatomy than most gynecologists. She also discovered that her aunt had robbed her trust account of almost eighty thousand dollars, making it impossible for her to go to college.

As things turned out, getting a job at a large factory specializing in electronic equipment was the best thing that could have happened to her. In less than five years, she was a unit supervisor. Two years later, she was promoted to Quality Control and transferred to the corporate home office. Her supervisor was none other than Sylvie. They reconnected almost instantly and had been together ever since.

Snuggling closer, Sylvie nuzzled Angie's neck contentedly. Whatever hardships they had endured, the rewards far outweighed the pain.

Angie glanced down at the head resting on her shoulder and lightly ruffled Sylvie's dark blonde hair. A slight movement on the wall caught her attention. She glanced toward the shadows. For a second she thought she saw them shift on their own as if they were readjusting their positions to get more comfortable...much like she and Sylvie had done a few minutes earlier. Blinking several times, she shook her head and then dismissed it.

Damn, I'm getting as bad as Sylvie, she thought. Closing her eyes, she moved Sylvie's head off her shoulder and onto a pillow, then rolled onto her side. Careful not to bump Sylvie's injured shoulder, she snuggled against her lover until they lay spooned together. Kissing the back of Sylvie's neck, Angie settled into a quiet slumber, sensing her partner was already asleep. Neither had turned the light off.

* * *

The two Shadows waited patiently for their human counterparts to fall asleep. Once they were assured they wouldn't be noticed, they hugged each other gleefully.

Playtime, Angie's Shadow Soleil, whooped, jumping up.

Your human is so serious. Why are you two so different? asked Lumiere, reaching out to touch the soft darkness of her Shadow-partner.

I balance her!

Has she always been this way? I mean before we met.

Yes, but she's better now. There was a time when I thought I'd lost her, Soleil said, reaching out to stroke her life-partner's hair. Sylvie's Shadow shuddered. Losing one's life-partner was the worst thing that could happen to a Shadow. *No, no! I don't mean detachment. I meant mentally. When her mother died, she blamed herself,* Soleil said, feeling Lumiere's reaction.

Why?

It's a human thing.

How sad. Why would Angie blame herself? Lumiere stared at Angie's sleeping form as Soleil continued running her shadowy fingers through her soft hair.

Humans are strange that way, Soleil said. *"They take on burdens that aren't theirs to bear. This one wasn't hers but there wasn't any way for her to know that. Her mother and her mother's life-partner were out of sync. Colleen was depressed and thought she was going crazy when she heard voices. It was only her life-partner trying to help her. I tried to warn Luce but she wouldn't listen. Afterward, all I could do was focus on Angie and hope I wasn't repeating Luce's mistake. Fortunately, you and Sylvie came into our lives.*

Lumiere snuggled closer to Soleil before responding to her Shadow-partner's comment.

I felt your pain and wondered what was causing it. My human has always been close to me. She picked up on my thoughts and was curious too. When she saw Angie, she was immediately drawn to her essence, just as I was to yours. We both wanted so badly to soothe your pain.

You did. Angie's a great person...very compatible with your life-partner — like us, Soleil said.

That's so true! Speaking of us, are we going to talk all night or take advantage of the light they left on?

Like you really need to ask? By the way, you realize that was intentional.

Yeah, Angie may not admit it, but she's beginning to believe in us. Next thing you know, she'll be talking to us like Sylvie.

Soleil laughed at the thought. She seriously doubted Angie would ever truly believe in *Les Gris.*

I doubt that. Besides, they couldn't afford the electric bills if they left the lights on all night, every night.

And we'd never get any rest!

Giggling, Lumiere and Soleil began wrestling playfully and then collapsed against each other. Slowly, they explored each other's darkness, savoring the intimacy of a touch that only

Shadows could truly appreciate, and then, because even Shadows had limited energy reserves, they snuggled together and slept.

CHAPTER 8

The Child

THE STREETS WERE dark and mostly vacant. Occasionally, someone would walk by and glance at the small group of people huddled under the streetlight on the corner. They were a strange-looking gathering. Three men surrounded a woman who was talking to them in a low voice. From all appearances, she seemed to be reprimanding them. Heads bobbed up and down vigorously. Small whimpers could be heard through the stillness of the night. One passerby stopped, his curiosity and libido aroused by the woman's unusual looks.

With flaming red hair and deep, copper-colored skin, she stood barely five feet tall. A black tank top showed enough cleavage to be enticing, but fell short of being indecent. Silver Capri slacks displayed a sleek trim figure with long legs, slim ankles and cloven-hoofed feet. The man blinked several times and rubbed his eyes. When he glanced back down, he saw neatly trimmed toenails peeking out of the end of silver sandals.

"I must be more tired than I thought," he mumbled and walked away scratching his head. "Too bad. I bet she's a good fuck!" Had he looked back, he would have seen several pairs of bright red eyes staring coldly at his departing figure. Jack

Henry had just won the trip of a lifetime and his journey was about to begin.

Nodding her head in his direction, the woman directed the short, balding man to her right to follow him.

"You know what to do — and Dagon, make sure Soulkeeper knows he's mine."

"Yes, mistress," Dagon replied and bowed slightly. Rubbing his hands together gleefully, he trotted after the human. The demon hadn't taken a mortal soul in over two hundred years. If he was lucky, the Child would let him have it after she tired of her newest plaything.

"I should be the one to take him," grumbled Paymon and then flinched at the icy glare burning into his own protected core.

Demons didn't have souls. Instead their inner being held a core of energy fueled by the fires of the Underworld. As long as those fires burned, the demons were relatively safe from other demons. They weren't, however, completely immune, especially to those in the upper caste of the demon world. The more powerful the demon, the more pain it could inflict on subordinates. Immortality didn't guarantee a pain-free existence.

Dis, their Underlord and sovereign ruler, showed little interest in the day-to-day lives of the inhabitants. As long as everyone obeyed his rules, he allowed them to go about their business undisturbed, leaving the order and discipline to his commanders. Few dared to anger or alienate the Elite of Hell.

Still, although they considered themselves immortal, many demons had disappeared over the millennium. Some were lost in the Great Battle with Dis' Twin while others simply vanished. Few dwelled on this fact. Demons didn't want to think about their vulnerabilities.

"I have a more important job for you," the woman said, turning back to her companions. Her voice was whispery soft, but cold and emotionless. Paymon nodded obediently. The third demon remained silent. It wasn't wise to interrupt the Child. As the daughter of Dis and Lilith, she was more powerful than all the lesser demons of the Underworld and most of the Elite. Some thought she might one day displace her sire and become supreme ruler of their realm. "I am looking for something...something special."

"Name it, mistress, and we will find it," Paymon promised, rubbing his hands together in anticipation. Staying in the good graces of the Child would ensure his protection from other demons.

The Child stood quietly for a few seconds. She knew what she was about to say could jeopardize her position with her followers. Being ambitious, demons were opportunists, switching loyalties whenever it benefited them. That didn't mean all demons suffered this affliction. Many understood the true meaning of loyalty, especially those of the Elite. Loyalty created order, and order provided unlimited resources and power.

The Child understood this. She was next in line to ascend the throne, should her father die. Even though he had sired many demons, none of them were as powerful or as intelligent as she. Unfortunately, Dis was immortal. Not even his Twin, the master of the Overworld, had the power to destroy him.

Still, all things had weaknesses. Discover the Underlord's, and the Child could bring about his fall or demise, not that she was eager to have her sire killed. Condemning him to the Netherworld, like he had done to her, would be a fitting punishment.

The demoness shook her head, banishing those thoughts for the moment. Until she recovered what she had lost, she wouldn't be able to hold her own loyal demons for long.

"Mistress?" Paymon whined, nervously.

The Child stared into the beady red eyes of her servant. Bright orange and black flames danced frantically up and down, a sign of his nervousness.

"Are you afraid of me, Paymon?"

Paymon swallowed. To deny it would be foolish. The Child knew what he was feeling. She was of The Blood, which gave her powers he could only dream of. Lying would make her distrust him more, and Paymon needed to be trusted. It was his only way to move to a higher caste. She was his one hope for improving his status amongst the other demons.

"Ye...yes," he stammered.

"Good! You should be. I will destroy you if you ever betray me."

The calmly spoken words made him shiver. Swallowing, he nodded.

"But follow me, obey me and serve me faithfully and I will give you power and status. You will be an Elite and among the highest of our order."

"I am yours to command, mistress. Tell me what you need."

"I need my Shadow." It was said so matter-of-factly — no emotion, no embellishments.

Paymon blinked.

"You...your shadow?"

Glancing down, he noticed the gray distorted image that spread faintly across the sidewalk beneath the streetlight.

"There is your shadow," he said, pointing at the concrete slab.

The Child laughed. Although it was a pleasant sound, he shivered again.

"That is nothing! Merely an illusion."

"I...I don't understand, mistress."

"No doubt! That's nothing more than a shell of my shadow. I am missing its essence. I must find it."

Paymon was confused. Was she losing it? Had her time in the Netherworld driven her insane?

"No, I'm not insane," the Child replied, answering his unspoken thoughts.

Paymon blanched, afraid she had read his thoughts.

"And no, I'm not reading your thoughts," she added. "You're very transparent. Now, we've wasted enough time. Listen carefully and you'll understand. Shadows are more than just the result of objects blocking light. They are live energy dependent on light and their host. The two complete each other. Without both parts joined, each becomes significantly less than the whole."

"How do you know this?" Paymon asked, his curiosity overriding his fear.

Normally, she would have rebuked him for questioning her about anything, but the demoness understood how absurd her explanation sounded. Even she had found it difficult to accept. Had she not felt its essence waiting for her at the moment she transitioned from the Netherworld to the Underworld, and then ripped away, she wouldn't have believed it. Too excited at being released from her prison, the Child had ignored the empty feeling that assailed her. Only later did she realize that something was horribly wrong. By then it was too late. Her *Les Gris,* her *Shadow*, was gone.

* * *

I never even knew you existed, she thought, remembering back to that moment. *I had assumed it was a mortal thing.* She had learned of the *Les Gris* while trapped in the Netherworld. Through the invisible barrier that separated her prison from freedom, she had grown aware of them and their importance. The knowledge could give her an edge over demons and humans if she were able to escape. Unfortunately, what she once considered a weakness in others was now threatening her own existence even more. She was slowly losing her sanity.

"What happened to your shadow?" the third demon asked timidly, and then flinched when she glared at him angrily. He had been quietly listening, not wanting to interrupt the Child, but his curiosity got the better of him, too.

The demoness reigned in her unreasonable anger as she turned to stare at Nybbas. Although a minor demon, he was a master of dreams and visions. This made him a valuable asset in her arsenal. With some coaxing, she would be able to use his abilities to affect mortal and demon, or anything that dreamed.

Even Father dreams, she thought, refocusing on her ultimate goal. *But I'll worry about that later. I need to solve my present problem.* The little demon eyed her nervously, hoping he hadn't angered his mistress. "It's alright, Nybbas," the Child said, calming her growing madness. "It was somehow stolen as I re-entered the Underworld. I need to find out what happened."

"Maybe it's just lost," Paymon offered. "We can look for it. You want we should start looking?"

"It's not lost. Shadows don't just get lost. At least not mine. It was stolen," the Child replied. The coldness in her voice warned him not to push her too far.

Swallowing nervously, Paymon decided to try another suggestion. "You think a mortal took it?" The thought that such a thing could happen was disturbing to Paymon. Humans were supposed to be weak.

"I don't know, but I doubt it. I know of no mortal this powerful. It's something else."

"What else could it be?"

Before she could answer, Nybbas hissed loudly. The demoness and Paymon turned in unison to stare at the normally timid minion.

"Me sor...sorry, mistress," he squeaked, terrified he had angered her.

"I'm not angry, Nybbas. Have you thought of something?"

Nodding his head rapidly, he looked around to see if anyone might be listening. Satisfied, he leaned close to her ear and whispered.

"Me see things sometimes. Others, they think me crazy, but me not crazy."

"No, you're not crazy. I know you have special gifts. What have you seen?"

Moving physically closer, he again checked his surroundings and clicked his tongue nervously.

"Darkness! Me see darkness."

"Darkness? I don't understand."

"Kobal. He once high demon. Now he nothing. Crazy. Laugh all time. Happy dance. Demons no happy dance."

"What does that have to do with darkness?"

"Don't mind him, mistress. He's always been a little off," Paymon said, disgustedly.

"Me not off. I see darkness surround Kobal one night. Like invisible cloud, but I see it. Kobal never same again."

The Child wasn't sure what to think about Nybbas' revelation. As a master of visions and dreams, it was possible he suffered a form of dementia or at least lost touch with reality on occasion. Still, much of what he saw was real.

"What do you mean by invisible cloud?"

"Me see cloud but it not there. Think it not real but it real alrighty. It surround Kobal. Kobal not see but Kobal change after. Kobal laugh at everything. No take serious anything. Happy, happy. Feet dance all the time. Invisible cloud steal his essence."

The demoness wasn't sure whether or not to believe the small minion. If what he had seen was real, then it could be what had happened to her.

"Is that the only time you've seen this cloud?"

Nybbas hesitated before answering. Fidgeting, he wasn't sure how much more to reveal.

"No...me see one time before. In vision."

"In a vision? What vision?"

Again, Nybbas hesitated. Looking frantically around, he shifted uncomfortably.

"Nybbas!"

"Me have vision of you leaving Netherworld. You appear, cloud appear and then gone. Me no think important. Think crazy dream is all."

The information was all she needed to convince her that Nybbas' vision was real. As hard as it was to believe, something had managed to separate her from her Shadow before it had re-attached. If she didn't recover it soon, she could eventually lose her mind or at best be considerably weakened. Her plans of a coup over Dis would ultimately fail.

"I must find out more about this cloud. Paymon, return to the Underworld and see if any of your contacts know anything about this."

"Yes, mistress."

"And, Paymon..."

"Yes, mistress?"

"Be discreet. No one must know about this."

Nodding, Paymon walked into the darkness and disappeared.

"Nybbas, come with me. I need to talk with Mother."

Nybbas bowed slightly and followed the demoness. He had heard of Lilith but had never met her. As Dis' ex-wife and the Twin's creation, she was legendary in the Underworld. Some believed her to be even more powerful than the Underlord, if she had been ambitious. Fortunately for Dis, she wasn't.

CHAPTER 9

Lilith

LILITH WAS JUST putting away her books when she felt the air vibrating around her. Knowing few dared to enter her office without announcing themselves, she was curious about who was that brazen. She didn't have long to wait.

"Good evening, Mother."

"Caelene. What brings you here?"

Lilith hadn't seen her daughter for a while. The Child had refused her invitations to spend time in the mortal world under the guise of wanting to renew her life in the Underworld. Lilith knew there was more to it than that but decided not to press the issue. She was long past exercising her maternal rights over her rebellious daughter.

"I seek your wisdom," Caelene said. "Forgive me if I am intruding at an inopportune time."

"I will always make time for you. It must be extremely important to bring you here."

Her daughter gave a faint nod.

Looking past Caelene's waist, Lilith nodded at the small minion trying to hide behind the Child. His expression was a mixture of sheer terror and awe.

"You're keeping strange company these days, or do you feel the need for a bodyguard now? I must warn you, I don't like uninvited guests here, excluding you, of course."

Turning to look at the cowering servant, Caelene flipped her hand in a dismissive manner.

"He's harmless and I'd like him to stay, with your permission, of course." Fearful that he had angered Lilith, Nybbas was about to vanish when Caelene stopped him. "You stay." Turning back to her mother, she explained. "His presence is needed."

Lilith's eyebrows shot up in surprise. Nybbas was a minion who, because of his unique ability for having visions, had been raised to the status of minor demon. For Caelene to admit to needing him was intriguing. Deciding not to comment, she motioned for her two guests to sit.

"So, what can I do for you?"

"I...I have a problem."

The hesitation and admission surprised Lilith. Standing, she walked around her desk and leaned her hips against it. Looking down into her daughter's fiery, reddish-brown eyes, she searched for something that would explain Caelene's discomfort, but found nothing. The Child would say what was bothering her at her own pace.

For several minutes, there was only silence. Finally, Caelene spoke.

"Something is wrong with me."

"Wrong?"

"Yes. I knew it upon my return. Something didn't feel right, but I couldn't figure it out...until recently."

"What is it?" Lilith asked, her forehead furrowed as she concentrated on her daughter's expressionless face. *Will you ever lose that control?* She thought. Lilith already knew the answer but refused to give up hope. Caelene was the product of

Dis' and her mismanagement and misunderstandings. They had only themselves to blame for their daughter's stoicism and distant nature.

Caelene resented Lilith's failure as a mother, not understanding the reason behind it. Dis' brother, the Twin, had created Lilith to be Adam's wife. When Lilith rebelled against Adam's attempts to make her submissive, Dis came to her rescue. Although his motives were selfish, he enjoyed her company and obvious intelligence.

In time, Lilith became pregnant, much to the chagrin of both of them. Unfamiliar with the concept or process, Lilith failed miserably at bonding with her unborn child and then caring for her afterward. Angry at being shuffled aside, Caelene believed that had Lilith stayed with Adam, her own life would have been better.

As illogical as it seemed, the Child took out her resentment on Adam and his new wife, Eve. When she destroyed their innocence, both Lilith and Dis banished her to the Netherworld. It was only recently that she was released to return to the home she knew.

* * *

Turning to Nybbas, Caelene nodded.

"She miss Shadow essence, Mistress Lilith," the minion yelled excitedly and then slapped his hand over his mouth. Always nervous, sitting with the Underworld's most legendary demoness was almost unbearable. "Sorry," he whispered and gulped.

"Don't be afraid, Nybbas. Explain what you mean, please," Lilith ordered softly.

"Invisible cloud. It steal Shadow. I see in dream."

"I still don't understand. What invisible cloud? What dream?"

Nybbas sighed. Talking wasn't his strong point and this was more difficult than normal.

"Child no have Shadow essence. Cloud steal it when she enter Underworld. She no complete now. No whole. Unbalanced."

Looking from the minor demon to her daughter, Lilith wasn't sure what to say. The whole story sounded bizarre, but Nybbas' visions and interpretations were rarely wrong, and Caelene wouldn't have brought him with her if she didn't believe it.

"This doesn't make sense. What is a shadow essence and how can anything steal it? Even if it did, I don't see how you would be affected by that."

"Trust me, mother. I've seen the effects this has had on humans when I was in the Netherworld. They go insane. It's slowly happening to me. I can feel the madness crawling around in my mind."

Lilith caught her breath. Such an admission from Caelene emphasized the seriousness of the situation. She would never allow another to know of her weaknesses.

"Could it be just the result of your time spent in the Netherworld? No one has ever returned from there so you may just be feeling a residual effect."

Caelene shook her head. She had considered the possibility but knew better.

"I believe Nybbas, mother," she said in a flat voice. I was hoping you had heard of this before and could help."

"I've never heard of such a thing. Nybbas, is there anything else you can tell me about this *cloud*? You said it was invisible. How could you see it?"

61

"In dream. I see all in dream. Even that I can't see visible. I see cloud steal Kobal's essence."

"Kobal's?"

Lilith was stunned. She had known this particular demon well. Although once he was one of the high demons, entertaining the soldiers of Dis' Legions, now he was a babbling idiot, dancing through the Underworld like a marionette. Whatever had happened to him had been instantaneous and unexplainable.

Some demons were insane or had limited mental capabilities, but it was rare for a sane one to develop such an extreme mental disorder. If something could steal a high demon's Shadow and drive him to madness, every demon could be in danger. The question was, what sort of danger? More importantly, what could anyone or anything do about them? Caelene was too powerful a demoness to let this happen to her easily.

"This is extremely troubling. If what you say is true, the ramifications could be catastrophic. Does Dis know about your visions, Nybbas?"

Nybbas shook his head. The Underlord had little interest in the minion's visions or dreams.

"Master busy. No time for lowly like me."

"Naturally. He's too busy entertaining himself with his guests. It's probably best he doesn't know right now. No use getting him excited. We know how he tends to overreact sometimes."

Nybbas nodded in agreement. Besides, it never boded well for the lower castes to draw too much attention to themselves, and Dis didn't look kindly on having his orgies disturbed.

Caelene also agreed. As long as it didn't affect him, her father wouldn't bother himself with his daughter's dilemma. She had always been on her own as far as he was concerned.

"I'm not sure what I can do to help you but I'll ask around. Maybe one of the other demons has heard about this cloud or missing shadows."

"I was hoping for more."

"More?"

"Yes, I know you have a connection with the spirits. I was hoping you..."

The Child hesitated. She hated asking her mother for a favor, considering their past. After all, had Lilith and Dis not condemned her to an eternity in the Netherworld, this would never have happened. Granted, her mother was instrumental in releasing her from her prison of nothingness, but it didn't make up for the thousands of years she had spent trapped and alone.

Lilith sensed her daughter's reluctance and straightened up to walk back around her desk. Sitting down, she clasped her hands in front of her and rested them on her ledgers. Leaning slightly forward, she locked gazes with Caelene.

"What were you hoping?" she demanded, dreading the answer she already suspected.

"I believe Intunecat might know something about this. Perhaps he is even involved in it."

"And what makes you think that?"

"He rules the darkness. He *is* the darkness. At the very least he may have knowledge of this *cloud.*"

As much as Lilith hated to admit it, Caelene was right. Intunecat was the Dark One, master spirit of the dark realm. He knew more about the things that lived in darkness than anyone or anything.

"I'll ask him," she conceded. "He helped you once already. I'm not so sure he'll appreciate a second opportunity."

"I want to go with you."

"That's not possible. He doesn't like uninvited guests."

"That has never stopped you before. I see no reason for it to stop me. He won't do anything if I'm with you."

Lilith knew her daughter was right but was reluctant to intrude on Intunecat's privacy. He protected his seclusion like a mother did her child. Few dared enter the dark realm uninvited. Then again, few even knew it existed.

"I won't impose on his hospitality in such a manner. You will wait here," Lilith ordered. Before the Child could answer, her mother vanished. Caelene grimaced and turned to Nybbas.

"Get Paymon and see if there's anyone else that might know of this cloud or be suffering from its effects."

"Yes, mistress."

Nybbas disappeared. Moments later the Child was also gone.

CHAPTER 10

Intunecat, The Dark One

HE WAS INTUNECAT, the Dark One, Ruler of Darkness, First Born of all of the First Born. His world was void of light, making it impossible for anything to exist for any great length of time, or so he believed. Only he could hear the music of the darkness or see the beauty concealed by the blackness, and only he understood true loneliness, a loneliness so powerful he had tried to overcome it by finding a cure. Instead he had created light, and within that light, other life forms sprang forth. They were the First Born, each guardians of their own realm, and from them sprang life. At least that was what most of the Spirits believed.

He, however, couldn't be sure since in the beginning he could only see shadows moving about. It had taken eons before he was able to enter the world of light. Because he was of the dark, he found the bright new realm uncomfortable. Intunecat would never be able to exist in it as he had hoped, but he accepted his fate stoically. It was enough that he could venture into it periodically, and from there into the newer worlds springing forth from the light.

One in particular fascinated him. It was a world that shared both the darkness and the light. One he could journey into at will for there was never a minute when at least half of it was not shrouded in blackness. There, he could move about freely. He also found creatures and things he could control, especially humans.

Humans were terrified of the darkness, making it easy for him to manipulate them. Toying with them provided both entertainment and an excuse to interact with the other First Born for they also had an interest in this particular world.

* * *

Mari was the oldest First Born in the realm of light. She was the mother of Gaia and creator of the land and seas, making it possible for life to exist and grow. From her essence sprang the beginnings of much of the life that now existed. She nourished and guarded each organism until it was capable of surviving on its own. Then she allowed life to evolve on its own, although she continued to monitor its progress.

One species in particular caught her interest and in time earned her love. Mari spent millennia nurturing them. When they eventually gave up their dependence on the sea and moved inland, she felt betrayed and withdrew into her own world, leaving the world of mortals to the other First Born who had also taken an interest in the young life forms that were evolving.

Sarpe, second oldest to Mari, became guardian to the reptiles and snakes, and in doing so molded them in her image. Ursa cared for the bears and they resembled her. Vyushir was fascinated with the wolves, foxes, coyotes and other similar species. She was particularly fond of the wolves, for they showed an intelligence and wisdom far superior to the others. And then there was Arbora...Arbora the light-hearted, the colorful, the caring. She accepted the guardianship of all that remained unclaimed. Plants and animals fell under her protection and guidance, although she rarely interfered with their growth or lack of. The world of mortals and all that sprang from its core lived and died as evolution dictated. At least that was what the spirits believed.

They understood survival of the fittest. Occasionally, someone or something unique would rise above the ordinary creatures and the spirits would take a special interest in them. Such was the case with Yemaya, descendent of Mari, and Dakota, descendent of Maopa, a spirit who was once human.

* * *

Since the beginning of time, Intunecat had believed he was the only resident in the Realm of Darkness and that it was impossible for others to enter without his knowledge or permission. To his dismay, he found he was wrong. First, the demoness Lilith arrived, and then a time traveler named Saira...but that is another story. Neither was entirely unwelcome. He lived a lonely existence, although his world was beautiful in its darkness.

A strange mysterious music wafted through the eternal night, the source unknown. Intunecat attempted to locate the origins of the sound but failed. Eventually, he gave up and simply accepted it for what it was. There were too many other mysteries to be solved.

* * *

The black balls had been a part of his world for hundreds of thousands of years. In the beginning, there were only a handful of them. Now, they numbered in the millions. He had no clue as to what they were. They drifted in the darkness like bubbles in the wind, only there was no wind. Occasionally, they clumped together for short periods and then dispersed as if something had sent them scattering. As the odd behavior became more prevalent, Intunecat's curiosity grew.

Reaching for one ball, he balanced it on his palm, turning it in all directions to examine more closely. Perfectly smooth, it glistened and yet remained impenetrably black. Tapping on it with a forefinger, he listened for any sound and found none. In fact, his finger occasionally passed through the object without disturbing its surface. Flattening his hand even more, he pursed his lips and blew. It floated gently away and then stopped, hovering in one spot.

"I will discover your secret," Intunecat threatened softly. The ball drifted closer, halting only inches from his face. Eyes narrowing ominously, he was about to blow on it again when he sensed another presence.

"A new toy?" a sultry voice asked from behind him. Smiling broadly, the dark spirit turned to welcome the intruder.

"Lilith! How good to see you, my dear."

"Thank you, Intunecat. It's been too long."

"Time has no meaning for me but, yes, I miss our chats. What brings you here?"

"I seek information and possibly your help."

Motioning for her to sit, he followed suit. Crossing his legs, he leaned back and interlocked his fingers on his lap.

"It must be very serious for you to bring an uninvited guest into my world," he replied, his voice cooling slightly.

"Uninvi —"

Before she could finish, the Child appeared next to her.

"I told you to wait!" Lilith said, her voice shaking with anger.

Intunecat watched the two demonesses, intrigued at the raw energy bouncing around them. Both were forces to be reckoned with, at least in the mortal world. In his, they were powerful, but harmless.

"I don't have time for manners, Mother."

"Then you will make it!" Lilith hissed. "You may defy your father and others, but you will find I am neither as tolerant, nor as understanding. Now, leave this place or —"

"Let her speak, Lilith. It must be extremely important for her to come here in such a manner. Sit! Tell me what brings you here, Caelene. It is Caelene, is it not?"

Doing as she was instructed, the Child let her eyes roam up and down her host's body. He was tall and slender, but she could barely make out his features in the darkness. It was disconcerting.

"You're not what I expected," she observed, leaning forward for a better look.

"What did you expect?"

Caelene wasn't sure. She had touched his mind once before when he had guided her out of the Netherworld, but the act had never given her a clear image of its owner. Even now, sitting just a few feet away from her, his face was shadowed by the darkness. She wondered why she could see the rest of him so clearly but not his facial features.

"What I look like serves you no purpose," Intunecat said, startling her. The idea of him reading her thoughts was unnerving. "Our minds once touched, remember? Now that you are in my world, the link is strong. I caught a few mental images from you when you crossed the barrier."

"Then you know why I'm here."

"Yes. You search for Shadows."

"Shadows? I search for only one shadow. Mine."

"So you say."

"Why do you say that?"

69

"Why come here?" he countered. "This is the land of darkness, not shadows. Besides, nothing exists in this world that I don't know about."

"Even you, Intunecat, don't know everything. No one knows everything."

Intunecat thought about the black balls. The Child was right. He didn't know everything.

"Perhaps, but I do know this. What you seek isn't here."

"Then where else I can look?"

The dark spirit bowed his head and stared at his hands. It was true the Child wasn't his responsibility, but his fondness for Lilith tugged at his conscience. Blood was blood, and she was of Lilith's. Reaching a decision, he first looked at Caelene, then focused his gaze on Lilith's face.

"If I help your child, there will be a price to pay."

Lilith nodded. There was always a price to pay, even between friends. That was life.

The Child glanced at her mother's face and then at the shadowy image of Intunecat. To be in debt to anyone was an unpleasant thought. Being in debt to these two made her skin crawl. They had the power to collect what was owed.

"Do I have any say in this?" she asked sarcastically.

"No!" Lilith replied, her voice only hinting at the anger she was feeling. She was still furious that Caelene had so blatantly ignored her order to stay behind. "You came to me asking for help. You disobeyed my order, and you arrogantly entered Intunecat's world without being invited. Already, you are indebted to us. I recommend that you not make your situation worse by being stupid."

The harshness of the reprimand not only stunned Caelene but was a warning for her to tread softly — for now. If she was going to get their help, she needed a more submissive attitude. It didn't make her happy but she had no choice at the moment.

"I am yours to command," she replied, lowering her eyes.

Amused, Intunecat made eye contact with Lilith, expecting to see a softening as she stared at the top of her daughter's head. Instead he was surprised. Her black eyes blazed, reflecting the full fury of the fires of the Underworld. Arching an eyebrow, he held her gaze until the flames cooled and then nodded his approval. This wasn't the time or place for anger.

"What do you recommend?" Lilith asked, acknowledging Intunecat's nod with a slight smile.

"For a start, I must know everything that Caelene can remember since her arrival."

Turning to the Child, he waited for her to begin.

"What do you mean by everything?" she asked, hesitantly. Her plans to de-throne Dis had begun. If Lilith knew about them, she would surely inform her sire.

"I'm not interested in your personal life or plans. Those I already know. They are of no interest to me."

Caelene shifted uncomfortably and glanced nervously at Lilith. Her mother's face remained expressionless, giving away nothing of her own thoughts.

"Alright. Ever since I escaped from the Netherworld, I have felt..." The Child hesitated, searching for the right word. "Incomplete. At first I thought it was just the aftereffects of being away for so long and that it would soon pass. It hasn't. Each day I feel myself disappearing."

"Disappearing?"

"Yes. It's as if I am losing myself. I don't know how else to describe it."

Caelene went on to explain what Nybbas had told her. Neither Lilith nor Intunecat interrupted her. When she finished, an eerie silence settled across the realm as if it was waiting for its master to speak.

Intunecat had long been aware of the Shadow People and their fear of a demon that was rumored to wander the darkness in search of their essence. He had always thought this particular demon might be the product of overactive minds. It was even possible that they had sensed Intunecat's presence whenever he wandered through the mortal world and attributed their losses to him. Since they were immune to his influence, he tended to ignore them. Perhaps that was a mistake.

Lilith and Caelene watched Intunecat's motionless figure. Both understood the need to remain quiet while the Dark One contemplated the situation. For Lilith, patience was easy. She had learned long ago that it paid off. Caelene, however, was different. Having been locked in the Netherworld for so long, she now craved instant gratification. Shifting impatiently, she glanced at her mother and instantly recognized the smoldering anger in Lilith's gaze. Ignoring Lilith's orders could cost her dearly once her problem was resolved. Caelene would deal with the unspoken promise when the time came.

Aware of the tension between the two demonesses, Intunecat pretended to clear his throat.

"I have come across Shadow People from time to time, but I have only a limited knowledge of their ways. Let me investigate this further. I'll let you know if I discover something of value," he promised.

As much as she wanted to, Caelene knew better than to push him or Lilith further. That he was willing to help would have to suffice. Standing, she thanked him and vanished.

"Her manners are atrocious," Lilith said, shaking her head.

"She's young," Intunecat replied sympathetically.

"Not that young!" Lilith wasn't willing to dismiss her daughter's actions so easily. "But she'll learn."

The veiled threat didn't escape Intunecat but he decided to ignore it. Whatever Lilith had in mind was between her and her daughter.

"I'll leave that up to you," he said. "Come with me. We have much to do and very little time." Beckoning her to follow him, he stood and melted into the darkness that surrounded them. Lilith followed his essence until he reappeared near an iridescent black obelisk.

"It's my looking glass," he explained. "I can see anything I want with it."

"Anything?" Lilith asked.

Intunecat gave Lilith an exasperated look.

"Almost anything. Apparently there are things I've overlooked recently." Turning back to the shiny object, he waved his hand once in front of it. Immediately, images flashed across the surface like a movie in fast forward. Occasionally, he stopped the action and carefully studied the events taking place. After several seconds, with a flick of his wrist, he continued scrutinizing the ebony screen in fast forward.

Lilith watched both him and the images flashing across the obelisk. Although she was able to catch each image, it was difficult to interpret what was actually happening. Patiently, she waited quietly to see what Intunecat was looking for.

CHAPTER 1 1

The Shadow Demon

ITS WORLD WAS BLACK beyond black, glistening with an unimaginable darkness. The inhabitants wandered aimlessly, helplessly lost in the emptiness of nothing. Although there were hundreds of thousands of them, each suffered an unbearable loneliness. They could neither touch nor see nor feel anything around them as they moved through the still blackness, and It enjoyed their misery.

"Yes, my children," It whispered, deriving great satisfaction from the sudden stillness as all movement ceased. They waited and endured the long silence, knowing that to do otherwise would only increase their captor's pleasure and prolong their own suffering. The laughter that followed rang of smugness and glee.

"Good! You're learning. Please me and you will be rewarded. I can be benevolent when I'm happy."

As if to prove Its words true, a light appeared in the darkness, illuminating all of the inhabitants. For a split second, each felt a moment of joy and hope, then found it quickly snatched away as they were once again plunged into an abysmal void, absent of light. To be given the one thing they craved the most and then have it vanish so abruptly created a depression and loneliness so profound many were willing to do anything to get the light back... and that was what pleased the Shadow Demon the most.

It had the power to inflict great psychological pain on It's subjects so easily, and It thrived on their suffering. The problem was like an addiction. It needed more and more captives to sustain It's own happiness. There were never enough inhabitants in Shadowland.

* * *

Summoning forth one of the denizens of Shadowland, It waited impatiently.

"What took you so long?" It demanded, although only a fraction of a second had passed.

"Forgive me, master. I came as quickly as possible."

"Next time, come faster," ordered the Shadow Demon, aware that it was impossible for the servant to move faster, but enjoying the fear emanating from the pitiful creature.

"Yes, master. I beg your mercy and forgiveness. I am your most loyal servant."

"I have told you before not to call me master. I am no male."

"Forgive me, mas..." The servant swallowed nervously. "I'm your faithful servant."

"I hope so! Betray me, and I will be extremely displeased, and you know what happens when I'm unhappy."

"Ye... yes," the Shadow replied. Once, the demon demonstrated It's power by destroying ten thousand *Les Gris* souls with a flick of It's hand. It was an act of pure indifference, leaving the survivors feeling both impotent and devastated. The residual energies of their lost companions floated around them like the radiation from a nuclear explosion. It was their own dark Chernobyl, a constant reminder of the power of their captor. The Shadow Demon laughed gleefully, well aware of what It's servant was probably thinking. It was quite pleased.

"As a reward for your faithful service, I've chosen you to perform a special duty for me."

"Anything!"

The servant's eagerness was gratifying.

"Yes, I know. I'm taking you with me to another realm. I have need of more subjects. You will help me capture them."

The demon could almost smell the suppressed excitement as the Shadow anticipated returning home.

"Don't think you can escape me once you're there. There's no place you can hide that I won't find you. The darkness is my ally and there is always darkness."

"No, no, I would never betray you, mast..."

The Shadow Demon smiled at the obsequious tone.

"You're very wise. It would be your last act. Enough talk. There is a particular Shadow that has eluded me for a long time. I must have it and the time is now ripe. Then we can gather others from the mortal world."

"We aren't going there now?"

The disappointment in It's servant's voice was so pained, the Shadow Demon actually shivered from pure joy.

"Do you dare to question me?" It growled, wanting to inflict more misery, and was instantly rewarded by waves of fear.

"No, no."

"I thought not. What are you called?" It could never be bothered trying to remember It's servants' names... and why should it? They were far too inferior to be given such consideration.

"I am Rumex."

Without saying another word, It grabbed its servant and left Shadowland in search of It's prey.

CHAPTER 12

The Society

SYLVIE WAS RUNNING late but wasn't too worried. The others knew her job made her schedule unpredictable. Being the departmental supervisor in charge of Quality Control meant putting in overtime if the work was backing up or if a serious problem arose.

Today had been one of those days. One of the company's employees decided to jump from a fourth story window just after the lunch break. Everyone was devastated. Thelma had worked in Quality Control for almost twelve years and she was well-liked. Lately, though, several close acquaintances had noticed a change in her.

Normally, Thelma was very outgoing. She loved to tease her associates about being lazy but was the first to offer them assistance if they needed it. Then, as if overnight, she grew sullen and reclusive. If someone asked if she was okay, she'd mutter something under her breath and move away. Only after talking to her fellow workers did Sylvie understand the seriousness of the woman's illness. The real tragedy was that Sylvie could have saved Thelma.

Rushing through the revolving door, she darted toward the stairwell and hurried down into the basement of the apartment complex.

"Why anyone would want to live here is beyond me," she muttered, tapping a sequential series of knocks on the door at the far end of the hall. "Then again, I guess if you're blind, it doesn't make any difference."

When Belle opened the door, Sylvie smiled and gave her a quick kiss on the cheek. Glancing down the hall over her shoulder, she waited a few seconds, then stepped inside and shut the door.

"Hey Belle, how are you doing?" Sylvie asked, taking her hand and leading her toward the living room.

"Really, Sylvie, I do know how to get around in my own apartment," Belle said. "I'm doing fine, thanks. I take it you still haven't talked Angie into coming to one of these meetings?"

"Naw! She still thinks she's a non-believer but Lumiere said Soleil is working on her. By the way, how's Lunara?"

"Still keeping me out of trouble."

"Yeah, right. More likely getting you into it."

"Be nice."

"I'm always nice. So who's here tonight?"

"Randi and Cheryl. Mallory called this morning to say she may not make it. We also have a new member, Thomas."

"Thomas?"

"A recent convert. I'll tell you about him later. Randi thinks he'll do better if he and his life-partner are able to interact with the rest of us."

"And Lighthra is okay with this?"

"Actually it was her idea."

Entering the living room, Sylvie greeted the two women and glanced curiously at the young man sitting quietly in the corner.

"Hey Randi, hey Cheryl, how goes it?" Sylvie asked, walking over to give them each a kiss on the cheek.

"Doing fine," replied Cheryl, a professional looking middle-aged woman with swept back blonde hair.

"That goes for me too," Randi agreed. "This is Thomas," she added, waving toward their newest member.

"Hi, Thomas. Nice to meet you."

Thomas nodded his head but refused to make eye contact.

"Don't worry about him," Randi said. "He's not used to being around people. Beamon's been more or less guiding him most of his life." She pushed her long brown hair out of her eyes.

Sylvie frowned. It didn't sound like Thomas and his life-partner were in sync. That could prove dangerous to everyone if the two were unstable.

It was necessary, Lumiere explained. *Beamon realized at an early age that they were de-syncing and Thomas was developing some psychological issues. He had to take control of Thomas before something terrible happened.*

So Beamon is the dominant in their joining? Sylvie asked.

He is. Beamon's willing to give up his control, but he needs our help.

Then why let him into the group now? Wouldn't it have been better to stabilize the two first?

No!

No. Although Lumiere didn't give a reason, her answer was enough. Sylvie trusted her life-partner.

* * *

"I guess we might as well get started," Belle said, motioning for Sylvie to sit. "Anyone have anything new to report?"

79

Sylvie quickly described the suicide situation she had encountered. Cheryl had nothing to report. When it was Belle's turn, she hesitated and then told them about Sammy.

"You've got to be fuckin' kidding!" Randi exclaimed angrily. "Belle, how could you put yourself in that position? You could have been attacked...or worse, killed."

Cheryl piped up as well. "What the hell were you thinking?"

"Come on, ladies. You know Lunara wouldn't put me in danger."

"Even she can't predict how de-syncs or the detached will act," said Cheryl. "That was irresponsible of both of you. I think I'm going to ask Solana to have a few words with Lunara. This is totally unacceptable."

Like that's going to do any good, Cheryl's life-partner, Solana, interjected. *Lunara can be just as stubborn as Belle.*

Maybe so, but neither of them would like it if we had done the same thing, Cheryl replied, exasperated.

Well Belle wouldn't, but my people are more adventurous.

Even with your life-partners' lives?

The question caught Solana by surprise. She had never doubted her ability to protect Cheryl. Then again, she had never done anything that had placed her life-partner in serious harm's way. Humans were fragile, making them the weakest link in the union under normal circumstances.

Lunara and I will talk, she promised, conceding Cheryl's point.

* * *

"Honestly Belle, I'm beginning to think we're following a lost cause," Sylvie said, deciding it was time to change the direction of the conversation. She knew nothing anyone said

80

would stop her friend from trying to save the *Les Gris* and their humans.

"Today a woman jumped from the fourth floor of her office building," she continued. "She was barely alive when I arrived. Lumiere said she was detached from her life-partner. Apparently they had been separated for several months. Something is causing this. It's like a fuckin' plague."

"I agree," Cheryl replied, "but until we find out where the *Les Gris* are disappearing to, there's not much else we can do other than try to handle each de-sync case by case."

"Yeah, and it's getting more dangerous with each one. It's only a matter of time before one of us gets hurt," said Randi.

"Or worse!" Sylvie interjected. Glancing at Thomas, she wondered what he was thinking. He hadn't spoken since the meeting had started. "What have you heard from the other groups?"

"They're experiencing an unusual amount of de-syncs and detached people. The *Les Gris* are disappearing without a trace," Belle continued. "You may be more right than you realize, Sylvie. Something is happening to them and we need to find out what. That's why I called this meeting. I want each of you to be especially vigilant. See if your life-partners can learn anything from the *Les Gris* they come in contact with. It's crucial we get to the bottom of this."

"I'm meeting up with a few friends next week. I'll put the word out," Cheryl offered.

"Good, and make sure they understand the seriousness of this. All of you be extra careful, too. Now, is there anything else we need to discuss?"

"Well," Cheryl said hesitantly. "I didn't want to say anything but...well, Kenny's been locked up."

"For what?" Sylvie exclaimed. "What did he do now?"

"He assaulted someone for flirting with his couch."

"Jesus Christ! I thought we had convinced him that thing's *Les Gris* wasn't compatible with him."

Cheryl shrugged. "Who's to say? Just because the object isn't alive doesn't mean its *Les Gris* isn't."

"Oh, please, Cheryl. Let's don't have that discussion again. Our own *Les Gris* have said they aren't. They should know," said Randi.

"They don't know everything," Cheryl retorted and then apologized to Solana. *I just don't write things off so easily.*

Not a problem. Objects do have Les Gris. Anything is possible, Solana conceded.

"Well, I'm for leaving him in jail for a while," Randi said. "Maybe we can talk the store owner into getting rid of that couch. Hell, I'll even buy it myself."

"You know, Randi, that's not a bad idea," Belle said. "It's more expensive than he can afford. If we have it moved to his apartment, he'll be able to have it to himself. Maybe it will stabilize him enough to keep him out of jail."

Randi shook her head.

I agree, Lighthra said. *Whether the couch's Les Gris is a living entity or not isn't important. Kenny thinks that damn piece of furniture is alive and he's in love with it. Isn't that really what we all are looking for?*

I guess, Randi said reluctantly. "Okay, how about we all chip in and get it delivered while he's in the brig. Then I'll go and bail him out. You all realize this feels pretty stupid, though. And one more thing! I'm never going to sit on that thing after Kenny gets home. Lord knows what he might be doing with it." Randi shivered at the visions flashing through her mind.

"Oh thanks!" Cheryl exclaimed. "I really needed that image."

Everyone laughed but agreed. Kenny and his *Les Gris* had detached several years ago. Since then, although he was

82

functioning fairly well at the furniture store, he had become attached to a full sized sleeper sofa. Had it not been for his ability as a salesman, the owner would have gotten rid of him.

As it was, his obsession with the couch occasionally made things awkward. Although he allowed people to sit on it, he became jealous if they started running their hands over the arm rests as they enjoyed the soft microfiber material. In the last six months it had escalated, but no one imagined it would reach the point of violence.

We're all in agreement with you. This may solve the problem until we can figure something out, Lunara said to Belle.

"Well, I guess that's that, then. Anything else we need to talk about?" she asked.

"I think we've pretty much covered it," Randi replied, speaking for the others. Looking at her watch, she quickly stood up. "I've got to run. Wendy's meeting me at Quentin's Steakhouse for dinner and I don't want to be late. I'll take care of Kenny tomorrow."

"Wendy?" Cheryl asked, raising her eyebrows. "What happened to Rachel?"

Randi gave her a mischievous grin.

"Nothing. I'm just testing some new waters."

"Slut! You're always testing new waters. One of these days..."

"Yeah, yeah. Well, I can't help it if the ladies think I'm hot."

Everyone laughed except Thomas. He had been quietly listening to the conversations without commenting.

What's wrong with him? Sylvie asked Lumiere.

Wait until the others leave. Belle will tell you, her life-partner answered.

Aren't you being the mysterious one! Sylvie teased.

Belle escorted Randi and Cheryl to the front door, giving each a fond hug. Watching her, Sylvie couldn't help but feel a deep admiration for the blind woman. She suspected that even if Lunara wasn't there for her, Belle would still have managed to live her life productively and independently.

"Are you alright, Thomas?" Belle asked, returning to her chair. Nodding his head, he gave Sylvie a nervous glance.

"Has Beamon told you about the other life-partners he's met tonight?"

"Yes. He assured me they were okay with everything."

"I told you it would be fine. You just have to believe in yourself."

"Beamon has been telling me that for years."

"Then listen to him. He's been a good life-partner for you. Now, go home and let him tell you what he's learned tonight. This is new for him too. He needs your help as much as you need his if you're to become balanced."

Thomas grimaced.

"Beamon doesn't need my help. He's taken care of me all of my life."

"Exactly! He's shielded you against everything. That means he hasn't had an opportunity to interact with the *Les Gris*. You can't imagine the effect that has had on him. Such isolation can be devastating for both his kind and ours. It's time you gave him his life back. Quit being selfish."

Belle knew she sounded harsh, but shaking Thomas from his apathy was crucial if he and Beamon were to become balanced.

Don't let her upset you. She only wants to help us, Beamon advised.

I know. It's just that...well...she's right. You've guided me all my life...made decisions for me. I've grown used to doing what you tell me. Why does it have to change?

84

You know why, Thomas. I've done all I can for you. We have to become more balanced if we're to survive. I know you're scared. So am I, but...

It was the first time Thomas felt the fear in his life-partner. Beamon had always been strong...strong for the both of them.

What's wrong, Beamon?

When his life-partner didn't answer immediately, Thomas grew more afraid.

Beamon?

It's okay, Thomas. Don't worry. We've come this far together. Just trust me on this.

Sure.

Thomas felt relieved. As always, Beamon would handle everything.

Why didn't you tell him? He needs to understand how serious this is, Lunara said. It was obvious from her tone that she was exasperated.

I know, but not yet. Soon, though.

It had better be, otherwise I'll have to do something. We can't let you isolate yourself again. How you managed this long without us is beyond me.

We do what we have to, but don't threaten me, Lunara. I may be tired but I'm not weak.

It wasn't a threat. Just good advice, and we both know what I can do.

And Beamon did. The *Les Gris* could be quite determined when they wanted to be. Still, it was rare that they formed such strong ties with each other in groups larger than three or four. Contact was normally fleeting because they were dependent on their life-partner's lifestyle. Humans, for all their socializing, rarely formed long-term social groups in large numbers. This limited the ability of the *Les Gris* to interact with their own kind.

85

* * *

After Thomas left, Belle invited Sylvie to stay for a cup of tea. Knowing Angie was working late, Sylvie was more than happy to sit back and relax for a few minutes. Besides, she still wanted to know more about Thomas.

Sitting down at the kitchen table, she watched Belle moving flawlessly about the kitchen. Minutes later, Belle placed two cups on the table, followed by a steaming teapot. After plopping down on the chair, she picked up her cup and draped her finger over the edge, barely touching the hot liquid inside. Taking a sip, she leaned back and sighed. Sylvie watched, fascinated.

"Does Lunara help you in the kitchen?"

"Naw, she hates housework and I don't need her to help me here. I know every inch of this place by heart. Besides, it gives her some time to herself. She doesn't get much of that, having to help me so much."

We help each other, Lunara interjected.

You know what I mean and don't deny that you do most of the work, Belle countered.

We've been over this before, Belle. We're equal. Without one there is no other.

"Did she give you a piece of her mind?" Sylvie asked, smiling slightly.

"When doesn't she? She's more hard-headed than I am."

"Yeah, yeah. So what's with Thomas? He doesn't belong here."

"Maybe, but Beamon needs our help. He's been protecting Thomas too long and is on the verge of de-syncing if we don't do something."

"Why bring him here? Why not balance them first and then let them join The Society?"

"There isn't time. If Thomas isn't stabilized soon, we'll lose them both."

"Okay, so what's his problem?"

"He's a borderline sociopath."

Sylvie inhaled as she was swallowing her tea and started coughing. Liquid poured from her nose and mouth, spewing over her cup onto the table. Amused, Belle pushed the napkin holder in her direction. It didn't take imagination to know what had just happened.

"How the hell can someone be a borderline sociopath?"

"Beamon recognized the disorder in Thomas at an early age. If he had allowed the boy to develop in the normal manner, Thomas would have injured someone. To protect them both, Beamon became the dominant and kept the child under control."

Wiping up the spilled tea, Sylvie wadded up the napkin and stuffed it in her cup.

"And what happens when we try to balance them? Thomas will grow stronger and Beamon weaker. It could make them worse off if we fail."

"I'm hoping enough time has passed that Beamon has modified his disorder some. Lunara thinks it's a possibility."

"Lunara may be prejudiced. She wants to help Beamon."

"You know better than that. Lunara would never jeopardize *Les Gris* or human if there was another way. Logically it would serve no purpose."

Reluctantly, Sylvie had to agree. A failed balancing of life-partners would ultimately end in tragedy for both. Humans and their *Les Gris* never survived de-syncing or detachment for long without suffering severe psychosis or neurosis.

"True. Okay, I'm out of here. Angie should be leaving work shortly so I need to get home and start dinner."

Getting up, she put her cup in the sink, gave Belle a hug and then left.

CHAPTER 13

The Seduction

SHE CRAVED LIGHT, Natural or artificial, it made no difference. Light gave her substance, allowing her to move about and touch things that normally were beyond her reach. Light was also an enemy, taking everything away as easily as it had given them — but it was preferable to the darkness.

The darkness made her invisible just as it made all of her people invisible. She could sense the presence of those around her but could not touch or feel them. Sound held no real meaning since she could neither speak nor hear. Once, a long time ago, she had been happy. That was before losing her partner. Now, she lived a solitary existence.

Her life-partner! How she missed her. The detachment had been sudden, leaving her confused and lonely. There was no time to prepare for the separation. One moment she was firmly joined and the next moment ripped from the very life force that had sustained her. Had it not been for her uniqueness and strong energies, she would have faded away a long time ago. As it was, she had waited an eternity for the reunion. Now it was about to happen and she was impatient for the joining. Like a storm brewing, she could feel the energies slowly building. Soon, very soon!

"Are you sure this is what you really want?" whispered a voice from the darkness.

"I've waited a long time for her. She is my life," the Shadow replied.

"You're mistaken. She was never that," said the voice.

"What do you mean?"

"Think about it! You have existed all this time without her. You don't need her."

"I...I..." The Shadow was momentarily confused. "Who are you? Why are you here?"

"I am your friend. We're both your friends," the voice said softly.

"Both?"

"Yes. But where are my manners? Rumex, say hello to our new friend."

"It is my pleasure to meet you, sister." Although the new voice was pleasant, the Shadow wasn't sure she cared for it. Something about it seemed obsequious, almost servile. She decided to ignore it.

"Go away!" she ordered, wanting nothing more to do with either of the intruders.

"If that is really what you wish, then we will leave, but at least hear me out. If, after I have spoken, you still feel the same way, we'll be gone."

Hesitantly, the Shadow acquiesced. It had been a long, long time since she had actually spoken to anyone. Her life-partner was still several minutes away from being released from her banishment. Listening would pass the time.

"Speak. I warn you, though, your time is short."

"Thank you. I sense that you don't like Rumex. Why?"

"You call him friend. I suspect you're more than that to him. He has the aura of a servant."

"Servant? That's ridiculous! Are you my servant, Rumex?"

Rumex laughed unconvincingly.

"I'm not a servant to anyone."

It was the truth. The Shadow Demon definitely wasn't anyone.

"See! But we're wasting your time, Shadow. I know you await the life-partner you feel you need. There was a time when I was like you, believing my very existence depended on another. Fortunately, I discovered the truth."

"You had a life-partner?"

"A long time ago. Like you, we had been separated for quite some time. I felt a loneliness that only those who have suffered a detachment can understand. Then I found the others. They too were alone. In time, more joined us and we found solace in numbers. Now there is an entire world of us."

"A world? What kind of world?"

"A wonderful world. Isn't that right, Rumex?"

"Yes, wonderful."

"It's filled with the lost and detached. Some have even voluntarily detached."

"Voluntarily? Why would any Shadow do that? It doesn't make sense."

"They were unhappy. Maladjusted to their life-partners. I can't imagine anything worse. It would be a miserable existence, don't you think?"

Candesca had to agree. Separation was horrible, but a maladjusted partner? She shuddered at the thought. Sensing her weakness, the voice continued.

"Once they found us, or us them, we experienced something we had never hoped for — a commonality and moments of great joy. Our pain began to fade until it no longer existed. It was a new beginning and now we are stable and self-sufficient. We no longer suffer as before."

"How did you find them, or they you?"

"Those who found us were lucky. We're well hidden, out of necessity, of course. One never knows who is out there waiting to snatch us away."

"Who would do that?" Candesca asked.

"Have you never heard of the Shadow Demon? It is legendary among human *Les Gris*, and greatly feared."

"Then why should I fear It? I am a demon *Les Gris.*"

"One can't be too careful. You asked how others found us or we them. I've made it my mission to help any of our kind who are unhappy. Rumex accompanies me out of kindness. He hates the thought of me being alone."

"That's all well and good for you, but I'm about to rejoin my life-partner. Soon, I'll be happy again."

"Do you really believe that? You've been separated a long time. Your relationship with this life-partner was always difficult. As far as she was concerned, you never existed. Not even as a child did she give you much thought. Most children are fascinated by their Shadows, at least for a few years. Naturally, you may rejoin her, but you'll still be alone. Come with us. I can promise you'll never be alone again. You'll be surrounded by hundreds of thousands of Shadows and will be cherished every moment you are with them."

It was tempting, she thought.

"Did I mention we have light in our world?"

"Light?"

"Yes, a beautiful bright light like you can't even imagine. Its colors are glorious. You'll actually be able to touch the others and they you. Do you remember what it feels like to be touched? The soft blackness caressing you, the coolness of dark fingers stroking your body as you begin to merge..."

Although it seemed like an eternity, she did remember and shuddered with anticipation. If only it were true...

"It's true. Let me show you."

Before she could object she felt a hand gently stroke her cheek and then glide down her neck to her shoulder. Being touched felt so good.

"You can have this and more," the voice whispered softly. "Come with us."

She could feel her resolve weakening. The touch was slow, seductive.

"But my...my partner..."

"She won't miss you. She doesn't even know you exist, remember? Let us be your family. Let me show you my world... *our* world. I can give you so much more than she can."

The air vibrated faster. Soon her life-partner would arrive.

"You must decide now," the voice urged. "Once she arrives, it will be too late. Think of the light and those who await you. Would you give up your one chance at happiness for someone who doesn't care about you?"

The voice was right. Her life-partner had ignored her. They never played the normal childhood games. She had been too focused on seeking revenge against those who had wronged her. Perhaps she would now want retribution for her exile. The more she thought about it, the more she realized that her life-partner's energy had been filled with anger and hatred. That wasn't something she wanted to live with again.

"If I come with you...if I don't like it there..."

"Then you can return and rejoin your life-partner. I give you my word. I'll even help you merge if you need it."

"Then..." She was still hesitant. The vibrations were overwhelming her.

"Say it! I cannot take you if you don't say it," the voice commanded.

"I...will...come."

The moment she said it, a black cloud surrounded her and she realized she had chosen unwisely. The laughter she heard was pure evil and foretold an unpleasant future. If she could have wept she would have when she saw her life-partner emerge from the mirror. It would be the last time she saw her.

* * *

"You lied to me," Candesca accused angrily. "The *Les Gris* here didn't come willingly. Where is the light you promised?"

The demon laughed at the Shadow's naivety. Flicking It's wrist, It brought forth the light, exposing hundreds of thousands of lost *Les Gris*.

"Lied? Is not the light beautiful as promised? ...and are these not lost Shadows like you?"

"You said they came voluntarily."

"I said some were maladjusted or unhappy and detached voluntarily. That's true just as it's true they've found something here they never had experienced before."

"Your words are one thing. You've deceived me nonetheless. Return me to my world."

"Now why would I do that? You're mine," the Shadow Demon replied, amused at It's captive's boldness.

"I'll never be yours. I belong to no one."

"The others felt the same way. Now they obey my every command." Turning to Rumex, the demon patted him almost affectionately. "Isn't that right, Rumex?"

The Shadow nodded sullenly.

"Then they are weak. I am the life-partner of the Child. Nothing you do can change that."

Again It laughed.

"I already have," It replied smugly. "In time, your rebellious nature will subside. I can withhold the light until you surrender. You'll be alone, just as the others are."

"Surrender? You don't know me, demon. I've lived without my life-partner for an eternity. I don't fear the darkness or loneliness."

There was a truth and conviction in her voice that made the demon hesitate.

"We'll see," was all It said, and then the Shadow Demon vanished, along with the light.

* * *

Staring into the darkness, Candesca sighed.

"I don't deserve this," she grumbled and then chuckled at the absurdity of the comment. "Well, I might as well check the place out. I may be here for a long time."

Wandering through the darkness, Candesca could feel the presence of others around her. They seemed so close and yet an invisible barrier separated them from each other. Their energies were strong and yet strangely subdued. Candesca recognized hopelessness. There was a time when she had felt the same.

"Can you hear me?" she asked one source of energy. When she received no response she moved toward another and repeated the question. Still no answer.

"This is going to be fun," she grumbled. "I know you're out there. Are you supposed to be part of my torture? If so, it won't work."

Silence! But one of the energies shifted uncomfortably.

"So, you can hear me! At least tell me your name."

A slight nudge startled her, making her aware that the darkness wasn't blocking all of her senses. Apparently even the Shadow Demon wasn't able to completely control all within It's realm.

95

"Can you speak?" Candesca whispered, not wanting to scare away the timid being.

"It doesn't like us communicating with each other," a voice whispered back. "It will punish us if It finds out we're talking."

"Punish us how?"

"It likes to taunt us. We're given light and then plunged back into the darkness."

"And that you call punishment? You should rejoice during those moments. Light is our life."

"Yes, and our hope. The demon knows this. It gives us hope and then crushes it."

"No one can give or take away hope. Only you can do that. What's your name?"

"I...I don't remember," the being said, sadly.

"How can you not remember your name?"

"I've been here a long time. I guess it became irrelevant."

Candesca was appalled at the comment.

"A name is never irrelevant. It's a part of you. If you can't remember your born name then create one until you do."

Time meant nothing to the inhabitants of Shadowland. Candesca waited patiently for her companion to respond to her suggestion.

"Well?" she asked, after what seemed to be a reasonable time period.

"I can't think of one," the energy replied, projecting abject misery.

"Then I will. Let's see. Tell me something about you. What's the last thing you remember before coming here?"

"Hiding. I was hiding from the demon. My life-partner was dying and in great pain. I was so afraid."

"Afraid of the demon?"

"Yes, and for my life-partner. She was old and unwanted by her children. There was no one to ease her into her next existence."

"Where were those from the other side? There's always someone to meet souls."

Candesca knew it was a Soulkeeper's job to catch and assign the proper demon to anyone destined for the Underworld. If the soul wasn't, then the Twin made sure one of his own guided it to its final destination.

When she received no response, Candesca pressed the point.

"You're not telling me everything."

The emotional sob caught her by surprise.

"I lef...left her," it whispered.

"Left her? I don't understand."

"She wasn't dead. I was supposed to stay until she passed beyond, but I felt the Shadow Demon's presence. It was looking for me and I was afraid."

"This creature is no demon. It only uses that name to terrify you and the others. How did you know of it, anyway?"

"I was warned by another *Les Gris*. He said it could sense the moment a Shadow detached from its life-partner and capture it if possible. He was right. I panicked when my human was dying and left too soon. Now I'm condemned to this place for eternity because I'm a coward. I should have stayed with Josie to make sure she passed beyond."

Candesca could feel the entity's sorrow, but felt no compassion for its predicament. Although she was aware of mortal *Les Gris,* this was the first one she had ever met.

I hope the others aren't as weak as this one, she thought. Spending an eternity without Caelene was painful beyond imagination, but she was surviving. Listening to this Shadow whining about its cowardice would be unbearable.

"Most likely she passed on even if you weren't there," Candesca said, her voice cold. "Even if she didn't, it's a little late to do anything. Apparently you haven't learned from your cowardly departure."

"That isn't very nice," the entity muttered.

Candesca snorted her contempt.

"Nice? You're pathetic. Go back to that dark, solitary existence you've been leading and leave me alone. I have no use or tolerance for weaklings. You can't even maintain your chosen gender. It's the least you could have done if you had cared about your life-partner."

The insult had the desired effect. The entity's energies became charged, an indication it was angry.

"I'm not a weakling. I made a mistake. Now I'm paying for it. Who are you to talk to me like that? Apparently, It captured you too, or did you join It willingly?"

Candesca realized the question was just a lucky guess but she still felt as if she had been dealt a mortal blow. The Shadow Demon had used deception. Candesca had believed It.

"You're right. How about we put all of this aside and figure out what to call you? Are you sure you can't remember your name?"

"I wish I could. I remember everything else but that."

"Perhaps this *thing* you call the Shadow Demon has something to do with your memory loss. It's a good way to maintain control. Let me think. What suits you?"

Candesca never realized how hard it was to name something. Demon *Les Gris* were born with their names so it was never an issue. Their life-partners were also born with names. Only humans seemed to assign names to everything.

"Sparky!" she blurted out.

"Sparky! That's an awful name," the Shadow said and mentally cringed.

"Good! Sparky it is. Maybe it'll encourage you to remember your real name."

She could almost feel the pout and chuckled.

"So, Sparky, can you communicate with anyone else here?"

"I've never tried. It wouldn't like it if we did."

"Alright! You mentioned earlier that It gives you light and then takes it away. What else can It do?"

"Isn't that enough? We live for the light. We are of the light. It knows we need it to exist."

"Don't be ridiculous! You seem to be surviving quite well without light. It's controlling you because of your fear and you let it. Has It done anything else to harm you?"

"Ummm, well, like I said, It prohibits us from communicating with each other."

"You mean like now?"

Sparky wasn't sure how to answer. The Shadow Demon should have stopped them from talking by now.

"Maybe It's just testing us?"

"And if It was, what else can It do?" Candesca demanded.

"I...don't know. I've been too afraid to find out."

"Then it's time we did. Let's see if any of the others can hear us. Maybe we can give this 'demon' more than It bargained for."

Sparky wasn't sure it liked the thought but needed to prove something to itself. Having failed its life-partner, it needed redemption. Another failure wasn't an option.

"Excuse me but...do you have a name?" the Shadow asked timidly.

"Candesca."

"Oh, that's a nice name. What happened to your life-partner? Is she dead?"

"No, demons don't die," Candesca replied.

"Dem...demons?" Sparky swallowed nervously.

"Yes. My life-partner is one of the most powerful demons in the Underworld."

"How...how did you two detach if she's so powerful?"

"It's a long story. Suffice it to say, we did. I was waiting for her return when this Shadow Demon tricked me into coming here. It will come to regret that. Enough chatter, though. We have work to do."

Sparky nodded and then laughed. The darkness made it impossible for Candesca to see the motion, but hearing the sound felt good.

Moving through the darkness, Candesca continued to probe for others capable of or willing to break the Shadow Demon's rules of silence. She soon realized, however, that of the hundreds of thousands, only a few could actually connect with each other. Of those, fewer than a hundred wanted to chance the demon's wrath.

It will have to do, Candesca thought. *Now all I need is a plan.*

CHAPTER 14

The Rebellion

ALTHOUGH IT REFERRED to Itself as a demon, in reality, It was something entirely different. It had existed at least as long as the light, perhaps even longer. Too much time had passed for It to remember It's origins.

It lived in a world of darkness secluded within a realm much the same. If only the Lord of Darkness had a clue, It thought smugly and laughed at the irony. Intunecat was fastidious about his privacy. Having the ability to conceal It's own existence and that of the captive Shadows was probably It's greatest feat.

Now, something was wrong and It wasn't happy. Several of the Shadows were openly defying the rules by communicating with each other. If this continued, the Shadow Demon would lose control of It's realm. Summoning Rumex, It waited impatiently for the servant to appear.

"What took you so long?"

Rumex cringed. Once there was a time he thought serving It would bring about his freedom. Now he knew better. The Shadow Demon had no intention of setting Rumex free. He was exactly what It had said he was, nothing.

"Did you really expect me to set you free?" It demanded angrily. "You are useful to me, but you can be replaced."

"What have I done to displease you?" Rumex whined. "I have served you faithfully."

"You serve me out of fear. You're weak and cowardly, which means you can't be trusted. Still, I find you useful. Who are those that disobey me and who is their leader? I must make examples of them."

Rumex hesitated. He was a coward, but he wasn't stupid. He would eventually have to return to the others and bear the brunt of their unhappiness. Although each Shadow kept a solitary existence, there were ways of enhancing the loneliness beyond that created by the Shadow Demon.

"Have you lost your tongue or suddenly gained a false courage?" It demanded.

Shivering, Rumex shook his head.

"Forgive me. I only want to please you. I don't know who these Shadows are except for their leader. No one trusts me."

"Give me the name. I will teach the others what it means to betray me."

"Candesca. Her name is Candesca."

The demon wasn't surprised. The Shadow had a strong energy.

"Bring her to me."

Rumex nodded and vanished from the darkness. Seconds later, he reappeared with Candesca. Circling her slowly, It sniffed at her in a display of contempt.

"I'm impressed. You have collected a few followers here even though I have forbidden it." When Candesca didn't reply, It grew angrier. "Do you really think you can accomplish anything with a few pathetic Shadows backing you up?"

Silence! It glanced at Rumex. Such defiance in front of a servant would make It appear weak.

I can't allow this, It thought, but wasn't sure how to handle the insubordination.

"Take her away," It ordered. "I'll deal with this later."

Rumex nodded obediently but already his mind was mulling over what he had just witnessed. For the first time, his master had shown weakness. Looking at Candesca, he motioned for her to follow him. When she refused, he rippled nervously. There was no way Rumex could force the Shadow to do anything it didn't want to. Only his connection to his master gave him power over the other Shadows.

"Please," Rumex begged, his voice barely a whisper.

Candesca realized she was jeopardizing Rumex's position with the Shadow Demon and relented. There would come a time when she might need his assistance. Nodding, she disappeared.

The Shadow Demon had not missed the exchange and understood its meaning. If It didn't do something quickly, more Shadows would grow bolder and join the revolt.

Perhaps I should send her home. I can afford to be benevolent. Yes! That's what I'll be! Benevolent!

Satisfied with It's decision, the Shadow Demon vanished, hoping to lure more unsuspecting *Les Gris* into It's web.

CHAPTER 15

Dementia

MAKING HER WAY UP the stairs, Belle tapped a monotonous rhythm on the concrete steps. Occasionally someone would stop to offer her assistance, which she graciously declined. Most would give her a curious look and move on, but one man in particular seemed determined to help her as far as the nursing home door. Not wanting to arouse his suspicions, Belle grudgingly accepted his offer.

Don't be such a grump! Lunara chastised.

Belle sighed.

I know, I know, she replied, unable to dispel the normal depression she felt whenever she visited her mother. *I hate this!*

There was nothing we could do to help her. You were too young to recognize the symptoms until it was too late. Even I didn't know that Shinette was so unstable. She hid her illness well.

I'm not blaming anyone, Lunara. We can't save everyone. It's just...

Belle couldn't finish the sentence. She didn't have to.

She's your mother. It hurts more. Guilt is natural when you've helped so many. Move on, Belle. Your mother wouldn't want you to blame yourself for this.

* * *

Opening the door, the man stepped aside to let Belle pass.

"Thank you," she said. "I really do know my way from here."

Realizing that he had carried his Good Samaritan assistance as far as he could, the man bid her goodbye and left, much to Belle's relief.

Glancing up from her desk, an elderly woman smiled when she saw Belle approaching.

"Good afternoon, Miss Belle. How are you doing today?" she asked.

"Fine, Mrs. Brogden. How are you?

"Well, I'm still able to get up in the morning and make it to work, so I guess I can't complain." Annie Brogden had worked at the nursing home for twelve years. Her husband had been injured in an accident and had been moved to the nursing home fourteen years ago, after the doctors had determined he would never regain consciousness. The home director had been so impressed with her dedication and caring personality, she offered Annie a job as receptionist. Seven Oaks Nursing Facility had been her home ever since.

"Your mom's been moved to room 324. It's a lot nicer than her old room — more modern and a little bigger."

"Thanks. Could you get someone to show me the way?" Belle asked. It was expected. Blind people always needed help, or so others thought.

"Come on! I'll show you," Annie volunteered.

After guiding her down the hall into another wing of the building, Annie deposited Belle in a chair by her mother's bed.

"You just call out if you need anything," Annie said, patting her shoulder before leaving them alone.

How does she look? Belle asked.

She's well cared for, Lunara replied. *Maybe a little thinner.*

Reaching out, Belle gently touched her mom's shoulder.

"Hi, Mom," she whispered.

At sixty-two, Tamara O'Reilly looked old and frail. Turning her head she stared at the stranger sitting next to her.

"Do I know you?" she asked, her lifeless eyes peering uninterestedly at the young woman.

"It's me, Mom. Belle."

"Belle? Belle who?"

"Belle, your daughter."

"Oh."

For a minute, Belle thought her mother might remember her. For a minute, perhaps she did. Belle would never know. Even Lunara couldn't help on this one. Connecting with a lost *Les Gris* was bad enough, but a mind destroyed by dementia was beyond repair. No sane Shadow would enter into such a dark realm for fear of becoming lost in the jumbled maze of chaos.

Of all diseases, dementia was the stealer of souls and memories. Insidiously creeping into one's mind, it spread its tentacles through the brain like an invisible malignancy. By the time it made its presence known, the damage was done and the battle lost. Now, nothing remained of Tamara but a ghostly shell housing the remnants of what was once a vibrant human being. Belle could do nothing to keep at bay the beast within. Even Lunara couldn't retrieve those scattered memories.

In Tamara's case, as in so many others, the mind couldn't adapt to losing its life-partner and was self-destructing. Alzheimers! Brain disease! Those were the terms the doctors liked to use in their diagnosis of dementia. Belle and Lunara knew it for what it was. Over the years, The Society had managed to help many of those unfortunate enough to lose their life-partners. It never resulted in a complete cure. Most led relatively normal lives, although they still acted oddly at times. There was no cure for absolute loneliness.

I don't think she's suffering, Belle, Lunara offered.

"But you can't say for sure, can you?" Belle countered, her voice barely above a whisper.

No, unfortunately.

The two fell quiet, each trying to imagine how horrible it would be to exist without their life-partner.

* * *

Intunecat stared at the young woman sitting next to the hospital bed. Rubbing his chin, he cocked his head slightly, unaware that Lilith was watching his expression with interest.

"This one may be able to help us," he murmured, more to himself than to the demoness standing next to him. "She lives in darkness but has a strong connection to her Shadow-mate."

"You can tell that just from watching her?" Lilith asked, seeing nothing in the woman's behavior to indicate such a relationship.

Without looking at Lilith, he nodded and pointed at a faint gray aura surrounding the woman's body. "I've seen this before, but only a few times. It took me awhile but eventually, I discovered what it meant."

"Which is?"

"All life arrives with a Shadow-partner. For most, the connection is strong enough to keep both stable. Occasionally, it's so weak it creates instabilities. Even rarer are those whose connection grows stronger as they grow older. These two are the strongest I've ever seen."

"Even if that's so, I doubt if a mortal and her Shadow-partner have the power to reunite my daughter with her lost

Shadow. We don't even know what happened to it, let alone how they can be rejoined."

"They will know," he replied confidently.

"So how do we enlist their aid?" Lilith asked. "Knowing how most humans feel about demons, I doubt they will jump at the chance to help one."

"Don't underestimate them, Lilith. Especially this one. She has an inner strength that would surprise you. Besides, she doesn't believe in gods or demons."

"Great!" Lilith muttered. "Even more reason to doubt she'll help."

"Leave it to me," Intunecat advised. "I can be quite persuasive when I want to be." The smile he gave her was so beautiful, she barely contained a gasp. If he could have that effect on her, she couldn't begin to imagine how a human could resist him.

"So I see," she acknowledged, her voice slightly husky. "You'll keep me informed of your progress," she added, although she knew it was an unnecessary comment.

Nodding his head, he chuckled as he watched Lilith disappear into the darkness.

"Interesting," he said and then vanished.

CHAPTER 16

A *Les Gris* Moment

SOLEIL AND LUMIERE watched their life-partners Angie and Sylvie snuggling under the blankets, exhausted from their passionate love-making. Within minutes, the two humans were sound asleep, their breathing barely breaking the silence.

I get exhausted just watching them, Lumiere joked, nudging the dark shape leaning against her.

Right, Soleil responded. *Since when did you ever get tired during sex?*

Lumiere laughed softly. It was true that she and Soleil took advantage of those times when they could be together in the light. Both were grateful to Sylvie for giving them those moments together, and for Angie for believing in her partner even if she didn't believe in *Les Gris*.

So, do we spend the next seven hours staring at our life-partners or do we take advantage of the situation? Lumiere asked, stroking her Shadow-partner's cheek. Had anyone been watching, they would have seen one of the Shadows shimmer slightly as if shivering.

It's been awhile, Lumiere whispered, leaning even closer. Her shadowy head merged with Soleil until they were one.

Yes, too long, Soleil replied softly, enjoying the essence of Lumiere's energy as it seeped through her own, spreading its warmth across and around her until both shimmered with an invisible glow that only they could see. Colors flickered wildly in kaleidoscopic spirals, exciting their passions to greater levels.

Light was their lifeblood, but colors inflamed their passions. Each basked in a radiance that if it were measurable, burned brighter and hotter than the sun they worshipped. Fortunately for those around them, their darkness not only contained the enormous energy created but shielded the world around them from its destructive power. Fortunately for all, it was a force that could never be tapped by others.

Soleil groaned as Lumiere's hand roamed across the surface of her physical form. Unlike humans, a Shadow's dark shell was extremely sensitive to the slightest change in air temperature, pressure or light, an evolutionary adaptation necessary for their existence.

Again the two Shadows shivered. Lost in their passion, neither noticed Angie's eyes opening slowly and staring sleepily at the dark images on the wall. Blinking rapidly, she rubbed her eyes with her fingertips and then pushed herself up on her elbow for a closer look.

"This has got to be a dream," she murmured, her voice slightly raspy.

Oops! Lumiere yelped, shifting quickly into a more neutral position. *I think we're busted!*

Soleil glanced at her life-partner and laughed.

She thinks she's dreaming. Reaching out her hand, she touched Angie's forehead. *Sleep,* she ordered quietly. Yawning, Angie closed her eyes and settled back onto the pillow, snaking her arm under the blanket to embrace Sylvie.

Now, where were we? Lumiere asked.

Giggling, the two resumed their previous activities. They knew they still had a few more hours to satiate their inexhaustible passions.

CHAPTER 17

The Visitor

BELLE WASN'T HAPPY. Although visiting her mom was always depressing, she knew this time was different. The dementia had progressed to the point where nothing was left of Tamara O'Reilly's essence. It was true what people said. People with dementia died twice. Sighing, she made her way home, unaware that someone was waiting for her.

Opening the apartment door, Belle took off her jacket and hung it on a nearby hook. She didn't need to turn the lights on, but did so out of habit and consideration for Lunara.

You have company, Lunara said calmly.

"Company?" Turning in a circle, she tried to figure out who was in her house without being invited and, more importantly, how they were able to get in. "Hello?"

"Hello, Belle!" a male voice replied. Moving forward, he touched her arm gently. Belle shivered, but not from fear. His fingers were unnaturally cool.

"Who are you?" she demanded, taking a step backward.

"I am Intunecat. We've never met."

"How'd you get in here? I'm not afraid of you if that's what you think."

The man's laughter was warm and unthreatening.

112

"Good! I'm not here to harm you."

He speaks the truth and he isn't human, Belle.

"Not human? What is he, then?"

"I'm a spirit," Intunecat said. "I take it your *Les Gris* is talking about me."

My people have heard of the spirit called the Dark One. He's legendary among us, although I never believed he was real. It appears I'm wrong. It must be important if he has come here.

"So it would seem," Belle replied. "So, Mr. Intunecat —"

"Intunecat, please."

"Well, Intunecat, why are you here? Lunara seems impressed."

Do you have to make me sound like a groupie?

Belle smiled.

"A friend has need of your assistance. Yours and your life-partner's, that is."

"You're a spirit. What can we do that you can't? Surely you have a lot more power than we do?"

"Normally. Unfortunately, the problem lies more within your realm of expertise than ours. Otherwise, I wouldn't be here. I'm really not into socializing with mortals."

Apparently not! That sounded almost like a put-down.

"I think that was a put-down!"

"Put-down?" Intunecat repeated, not quite sure what Belle meant.

"You know, insult! Your egotistical side is showing."

"Ah well, my dear, some things are undeniable. I am superior to mortals. That is a fact and is not meant as an insult."

He has a point!

"I suppose." Belle's agreement was meant for Lunara, but she realized Intunecat would think she was talking to him.

113

When he chuckled, she knew he understood what was happening and laughed. "Well, apparently there are a few problems even spirits can't solve."

"True. Being superior doesn't mean I have all the answers, especially when it comes to *Les Gris* and the phenomena of detaching. Normally, I don't get involved in these things but this problem can have apocalyptic ramifications."

Talk about an attention getter!

"How's that?" Belle really didn't know what else to say.

"Perhaps we should sit down while I explain everything," Intunecat offered and then took Belle's arm to lead her to the couch. "You may find the details hard to believe but I assure you that failure will be catastrophic for all the realms."

Once Belle was seated, Intunecat lowered himself onto the chair in front of her and crossed his left leg over his right knee. Leaning back, he glanced around the room, noticing how neat everything was. Although she was blind, Belle had several pictures of her family on the walls and some oddly shaped knickknacks on the credenza and end tables.

"Why do you hang pictures of your family around you if you are blind?" he asked, switching his gaze back to the woman.

Belle shrugged.

"I don't need the pictures to remember them but knowing they're here makes the place feel more homey. Being blind doesn't diminish my need to have such reminders."

"I see." Intunecat thought about the black orbs that existed in his realm and realized he would miss them if they disappeared. Perhaps the feelings were similar. "Do you miss not being able to see your world?" he asked. "I should think it would be hard to cope, even with the help of your *Les Gris*."

"Sometimes. Lunara more than makes up for my loss though. She's my best friend."

"She? I wasn't aware that *Les Gris* were gendered. Interesting."

Belle had never really thought about it. She had automatically assumed Lunara was female like herself.

It's unimportant! Lunara interjected. *We are what we are!*

"Does that mean you're not female?" Belle asked, frowning at the thought. Surely she wouldn't have a male *Les Gris*.

Belle! It's unimportant! We are what we are! Gender means nothing to my people, although we may refer to each other as he or she from time to time. It's mostly for the comfort of the life-partner. Now isn't the time to get hung up on it, Lunara admonished.

"You're right. It's a little late to worry about it, now," she agreed. "As far as I'm concerned, Lunara is a she," Belle said, addressing Intunecat. "But it really doesn't matter."

Intunecat nodded. He suspected that Belle hadn't really thought about it. That was good. Assuming that her *Les Gris* was female probably made it easier to accept in the beginning.

"I suppose we should get down to business. There are matters I need to take care of. Much of what I have to say will seem unimaginable but I assure you, all that I say is very real. You and Lunara are about to begin an adventure that few humans have experienced. I hope you're up to it."

"We'll manage," Belle replied confidently.

Such confidence, Lunara teased. *Let's hear what he has to say first before we agree to anything.*

"I doubt we'll have any choice. Okay, shoot!"

Intunecat smiled slightly and then began describing the events leading up to his arrival at her apartment. Occasionally, Belle would stop him in order to clarify a few things, but for the most part she simply listened.

When Intunecat finished, he sat quietly for a few moments, watching the human as she processed all of the information.

Obviously, she was conversing with Lunara, although for the first time, she remained silent while doing so.

This is serious! Lunara said.

It's also beyond our expertise, Belle replied. *How in the world are we going to re-join a demon with her Les Gris? That's if we can even find it! Even with the help of The Society, we don't have enough power.*

We have no choice, Belle. Intunecat is right. This could destroy all the realms. I, for one, wouldn't want to battle any demon, let alone one that is insane. If she is the offspring of Lilith and Dis, then she is potentially the most powerful demon ever to exist.

Okay, let's say this isn't just a bad dream. Again, what can we do? We're going to need help.

Ask him, Lunara suggested. *He wouldn't be here if he wasn't willing to help, and surely the demons will have to pitch in.*

Belle nodded unconsciously.

"You know we can't do this alone. I mean, someone is going to have to find the lost *Les Gris.*"

"Lilith and the other demons are working on it, but I don't have much hope."

"You must realize we have less than a week before the Blood Moon! If we can't pull things together by then, it'll be several years before the next one."

"Yes. Unfortunately, your world wouldn't survive those years. Unlike us, you have nothing powerful enough to combat a demon such as she. The demons and spirits could hold her off for a while but it would wreak havoc on our realms as well."

Intunecat was startled when Belle suddenly jumped up. Lunara smirked but didn't tell her life-partner what had just happened. She suspected Intunecat would be embarrassed if

Belle knew he had flinched. Spirits such as he needed to maintain a sense of dignity.

"I'll have to call a couple of Society members. They may have some suggestions. Can you gather the others and meet me here later?"

"Certainly." Without saying another word, Intunecat vanished into a black void. Unaware that she was now alone, Belle continued. "Oh, and don't forget to knock before you..."

He's gone!

"Gone?"

Gone! Poof!

"Without a goodbye or thank you very much? That's rude!"

I'm sure it wasn't...

Before she finished her thought, the black void reappeared and Intunecat stepped back into the room.

"I apologize for my rudeness," he said, bowing his head slightly. "Until we meet again." And then vanished a second time.

There you go. Not only a goodbye but an apology. Problem solved.

Belle shook her head and headed to the phone.

CHAPTER 18

The Moment of Truth

BELLE HAD THOUGHT later meant hours, but instead it was less than thirty minutes. Without warning, Lilith and the Child appeared in her living room.

They're hee-er! Lunara announced dramatically.

"Damn!" Belle cursed.

Lilith laughed.

"Not yet," she replied, walking over to Belle to take her hand. "And it's not always as bad as you imagine. I'm Lilith. It's nice to meet you."

"Umm...Hi." Belle wasn't sure about the formality of addressing a demoness, let alone trying to interpret the odd comment. She liked the voice, though.

"You can call me Lilith. My daughter's name is Caelene, a.k.a. the Child."

"Hi, Caelene," Belle said hesitantly.

The Child glared at the human, willing the lifeless eyes to see...wanting the woman to tremble with fear at the sight of the fires that burned within her angry gaze. But it wasn't to be. Blindness was Belle's protector, at least one of them. The Child was powerful but she would have to expend a lot of energy taking on Lunara in her weakened state...energy she wasn't willing to waste on this particular battle.

"You'll have to forgive her. Obviously, her manners are somewhat lacking at the moment." Lilith could barely control the anger she was feeling. Enough was enough. Walking over to her sulky daughter, she leaned down and whispered something in her ear. Immediately Caelene stiffened but refused to make eye contact with her mother. Instead she grumbled a reluctant greeting, deciding that civility was better than facing Lilith's threat.

Good thinking, Lunara interjected.

"Lunara thinks you made a wise decision."

Ignoring Belle's life-partner, Caelene began pacing back and forth. With each passing moment, she could feel the instability growing and blamed her mother. Lilith had forced her to meet with the human when she had more important things to do. She and her demons had still not located her lost *Les Gris.*

"This is a waste of time." Turning toward Lilith, she glowered. "If I weren't a half-breed, it wouldn't have this effect," she accused.

"Apparently demons suffer the same end if they de-sync or detach. They may not have been a primary target of the Shadow Demon until recently. We can only assume humans simply serve its purpose better. Maybe because they are easier prey," Lilith reasoned.

Prey! The Child was appalled at the thought. She was a hunter, not the hunted. To think otherwise made her weak.

"I am *not* prey!"

"You don't like being a victim, do you?" Belle interrupted.

"Do not test me, human. I'm *not* a victim!"

119

"We're all victims in some way. You think because you're different that you're special? Look at you. If you're so mighty, why are you here now?"

"I'm here because *she* made me come," she said, pointing at Lilith accusingly.

"Don't be ridiculous! You're here because you need us. Have you learned nothing from this?" demanded her mother.

"I don't need your help. I am the daughter of Dis and Lilith. That makes me special. That is enough to give me the strength to overcome this minor inconvenience. It is only out of respect for you both that I'm here."

Perhaps it was Belle's blindness that allowed her to hear the fear behind the false bravado in the Child's voice. Still, she couldn't help but laugh at the arrogance.

Fire flared in the demoness' eyes but it wasn't Belle's laughter that bothered her. After all, the woman was only a mortal — but the mocking laughter of her life-partner grated. How dare... Caelene glared at Belle angrily.

"I can hear her!" She hissed.

We can be heard by some when it serves us.

"And laughing at me serves you?"

Yes. Your ego is your weakness. It will be your undoing. Already you are losing your way. Continue to play the fool and you'll end up one.

"I'm not...I mean, I can —"

What? You can what? Survive without your life-partner? Do what no other creature has ever been able to do without losing part of who they are? No, Caelene! You'll lose this battle. Does that not tell you something about yourself? You're weak when you're incomplete. You need our help and it will be a lesson well worth learning.

"Lunara is right," Belle said, again joining the conversation. "There are few options left to you, Caelene.

Lunara thinks we may be able to merge you with a human *Les Gris*."

Lunara had mentioned the idea to Belle after Intunecat left but hadn't been able to go over the details before the arrival of the two demonesses.

"No! I already have too much human in me. I'll not allow myself to be compromised by sacrificing more of me to a mortal. I'll prove all of you wrong."

Before Belle or Lunara could respond, the Child vanished.

Sensing the abrupt departure, Belle chuckled.

"She's got a temper."

"She gets it from her father," Lilith said. "I'll try to reason with her. There are very few options available now. Thank you, Belle and Lunara." Unlike Caelene, Lilith left through the front door.

Wow! She's a classy lady.

"Too bad the same can't be said about the brat."

She's young and barely in control of herself.

"Young?"

By demon standards, yes. Not to mention, she hasn't had much of an opportunity to interact with mortals or experience emotions. She has a lot of growing up to do.

"You like her," Belle accused, surprised at the thought.

I like what she can be, not what she is. Her life has been hard. She has every right to think she can go this alone after having spent what must have felt like an eternity trapped in loneliness.

"So you feel sorry for her. I guess I can understand that."

Lunara thought about it for a few moments.

No, I admire her. I don't know of any creature, mortal or otherwise, who could have survived what she has and kept their sanity. That alone is proof of her strength and it's that strength I respect and fear. If she de-stabilizes completely, I'm

*afraid many of us will be destroyed before we destroy her —
and destroy her we must.*

Belle had to agree. What complicated the situation even
more was not knowing which side Dis would take. It was hard
to believe he and Lilith would allow their child to be destroyed,
no matter how difficult she was.

"What can we do?"

*Unless she's stabilized soon, she'll be unreachable even for
us. I think our plan is the only choice but it's going to take her
consent and...*

When Lunara hesitated, Belle knew she wasn't going to like
what she was about to hear.

"And?"

And several may die during the procedure.

Belle frowned.

"I'm not sure she's worth the sacrifice. Wouldn't it be
better to destroy her before she completely de-stabilizes while
she's at her weakest? I know it sounds harsh but if she's as
much a threat as you think, now is the time to move. We can
deal with Dis and Lilith after the fact if there's a problem."

Lunara's mental snort was like a small explosion in Belle's
mind.

*You really are an optimist. Trust me when I say you don't
want those two angry at you or humanity. Not even God
himself could prevent the devastation they would reap upon
this world.*

"It was just a thought," Belle replied, suddenly feeling
guilty at even suggesting such an idea. "Tell me what needs to
be done to resolve this. We have very little time to act."

Belle patiently listened to her *Les Gris* as Lunara quickly
outlined part of her plan. Had anyone been watching the blind
woman, they would have thought her behavior strange as she
nodded her head, frowned and then nodded again.

"I don't like it, but at least it's better than doing nothing. I get the feeling you're not telling me everything," she said when Lunara finished.

Lunara ignored the last comment. She knew she needed more help than the *Les Gris* could give, yet she wasn't sure the one she had in mind would be willing to get involved.

Doing nothing isn't an option. I'll pass the information on to the others. We have only a few days before the Blood Moon rises. If we miss this one, it'll be several years before the next.

"I think I need to call Randi and get her over here tomorrow. I'll contact The Society members when I know a little bit more. Anyway, it's too late to call them tonight. Besides, I need a nice, hot bubble bath and a good night's sleep. I'm exhausted and I think you have something to do."

Belle knew she didn't need to tell Lunara how she was feeling, but it always felt good verbalizing her thoughts whenever she could. Having such an intimate relationship with a *Les Gris* sometimes made one feel almost schizophrenic. Belle did have the advantage of being blind, though. Without the visual senses, she was accustomed to hearing only voices.

Heading off toward the bathroom, she ran her fingertips slowly along the wall, an unnecessary action but one that she had retained over the years. Its solid feel always gave her a sense of comfort.

CHAPTER 1 9

Rainbow

LUNARA WAITED FOR Belle's mind to relax a bit before shifting her attention to her surroundings. Granted, the evening wasn't the best time to locate Rainbow, but as long as there was light, there was a chance the Elemental would appear. The mystical creature often dropped in to visit with Lunara and occasional offered her services when the Shadow wanted to treat her life-partner to a visual experience.

Where are you? I need you.

Within seconds a shimmering prism of light danced into the room, her rainbow hues glistening brightly in the dimly lit bedroom.

Lunie, how are you?

I'm fine, but I need your help.

Never one to stop moving, Rainbow continued her dancing, her vibrant colors swaying with a seductive innocence that fascinated Lunara.

How can I help, mon bel ami Gris?

Lunara laughed. The Boreal was a joyous creature and always teasing her, but the Shadow wasn't fooled by the superficiality she projected. Elementals enjoyed life to the fullest but like all living things, understood the seriousness of a world in environmental chaos.

For that reason alone, Lunara knew enlisting the aid of Rainbow and the other Elementals in assisting humans could be problematic. On the other hand, the whimsical creatures felt no animosity toward demons so there was a small chance they might agree. By nature they tended to be kind as long as something didn't arouse their ire.

A Les Gris has detached from her demon and cannot be found. We hope another will take her place.

And what does that have to do with me? Rainbow asked, swaying gently back and forth. *Demons don't interest me.*

I know, but this isn't a normal demon. She has the potential to do great harm to both humans and demons.

All the better, the Elemental replied, gliding smoothly away. Her colors began to flicker rapidly, an indication that Rainbow was becoming agitated. *The humans have destroyed most of us. It's only a matter of time before all Elementals pass beyond because of their foolishness.*

They're changing, Rainbow. Many have realized what they have done and are doing. They seek to save the future of our world.

Not soon enough for us.

Lunara knew the Elemental could be right. Time was running out for the *earth spirits.* If the humans didn't act quickly, the toxins would send nature into a downward spiral that would take Gaia hundreds of millions of years to correct. By then life would have changed so radically that humanity would cease to exist.

Do you wish my people to suffer the same fate as humans? Lunara asked.

Rainbow's movements ceased for a second and then she resumed her swaying.

125

I wish you no harm, Lunie. You're like a sister to me. We share the same need for the light.

True, but unlike you, the Les Gris also need mortals or demons to exist. They sustain us during the darkness. Without our life-partner, we're nothing.

Rainbow knew Lunara was right. Mortals and demons had a symbiotic relationship with *Les Gris*.

I don't know how I can help you. The Gnomes and the Undines have already declared Kryearah on humans. They will no longer help them as they have in the past.

Kryearah?

Yes, it means to no longer exist.

What about the others?

The Salamanders have much to gain now. They are the only ones who grow in numbers while the rest of us die. Even some of the Sylph have aligned themselves with the fire Elementals, causing great devastation.

And the Boreal? Where do your people stand?

They stand as they always have...independently.

Do you think they would help us? If we can't keep the Shadow Demon away, it may capture Raylena before the transfer is completed.

Raylena is the name of a human Les Gris. Do you really believe you can join her with a demon?

We must! It's our only hope.

I understand your dilemma, Lunie, but there's nothing my people can do. You said the transfer happens during the eclipse. The Boreal are of the light. Like you, we follow the sun and have no powers in darkness. Even if we could, what could a few Boreal do that thousands of Les Gris couldn't?

Lunara sighed, desperately searching for other ideas.

You're right, of course. I guess I was hoping for a lot.

126

Rainbow shimmered back and forth, her colors flickering like neon lights being switched rapidly on and off.

She knew that Lunie would never have asked her for assistance if the situation wasn't grave. Moving close to her friend, she flashed her reds and blues, while keeping the other colors still.

I may be able to get the Aurora to help.

Aurora? Who are they?

The night Elementals. I've only met a few and only on the edge of daybreak and nightfall. Only there can the two of us exist for short periods of time, but it's dangerous. Darkness will destroy a Boreal just as light will the Aurora.

Lunara felt excitement stirring within her. Since the Aurora lived in darkness they would be perfect allies against the Shadow Demon.

Can you find them quickly without endangering yourself? We have only a few days left before the Blood Moon.

I'll try but I can't promise anything. They're very shy and secretive but I know one of the places they hide during the day. I may be able to get a Sylph to help reach them.

You said the Sylph weren't willing to help.

I said some. I have a few friends among them. Besides, they love harassing the Aurora. It's almost a tradition.

Lunara gave a mental shake of her head. This was getting too complicated.

And I'm supposed to consider that encouraging?

It's not as bad as it sounds, Lunie. Like I said, the Aurora are very private. The Sylph can't resist letting them know there's no place they can hide that is unattainable. It's a game that's been going on for hundreds of thousands of years.

Alright, I guess I can understand that. No matter what they say, Rainbow, thank you for offering to help. It means a lot to me.

That's what friends do, Lunie. I'm off now. See you later.

Before Lunara could say goodbye, the Boreal was gone in a flicker.

"I guess I'd better see what Belle's up to," Lunara grumped.

* * *

"Where were you?" Belle asked as she pulled on a pair of old pajamas.

Visiting an old friend.

"Oh? Anyone I know?"

Belle knew the *Les Gris* had separate lives apart from their humans. Although she didn't know all of Lunara's *other* friends or acquaintances, her Shadow had told her about a few of them. There was one in particular Lunara seemed fond of — a light spirit named Rainbow.

Yes, I talked to Rainbow. She may be able to help us.

Lunara gave Belle a shortened version of her conversation with the Boreal.

"We definitely need all the help we can get. I'll keep my fingers crossed. In the meantime, a good night's sleep will do wonders for you and me."

For you, maybe. I still have work to do.

Les Gris didn't require much rest. They gained their energy and nourishment from the light during the day and from their life-partner at night. In return, they provided protection by alerting their humans to external dangers and keeping them balanced.

Sifting through the day's activities, Lunara carefully sorted each event and placed it in one of several categories. If she found an answer to a problem Belle was obsessing over, she made sure to save the solution. Other things were simply wiped away, leaving a jumble of memories that created weird but healthy dreams.

Once she finished "cleaning house," Lunara nestled down amongst those dreams to enjoy the strange rides on which they always took her. It was the *Les Gris* version of going to the movies.

CHAPTER 20

A Desperate Choice

RANDI COULDN'T WAIT to get to Belle's place. Last night's phone call had made sleep impossible. Leaving work an hour early, she caught a cab to her friend's apartment. As usual, Belle was in the kitchen cooking her favorite dish, meatballs and spaghetti. Randi's stomach growled ominously.

"You need to tame that rascal," Belle joked.

"It'll quiet down as soon as it gets a taste of that spaghetti. I don't know what your secret is but I have to say you make the best I've ever eaten."

"No secret, just a lot of experimenting."

Spooning heaping servings onto two dishes, she handed both of the plates to Randi and headed for the living room. Randi followed close behind. Once settled on the couch, they dug into their food. Belle waited until Randi was almost done before she brought up the reason she had called her friend.

Randi remained silent while Belle explained the Child's predicament. Putting her plate on the coffee table, she leaned back and rubbed her forehead. Neither of her *Les Gris* had spoken during Belle's narration.

"I'm not sure about this," Randi said. "Besides, it's really not my decision to make."

"I know, but it still affects you. You've lived with Raylena for a long time. She's become a part of you and Lighthra. Her departure would change all of your lives. It would be sure to create some instability."

How do you two feel about this? Randi asked her two life-partners.

The choice is Raylena's. She's the one who would be taking the greatest chance.

Randi and Lighthra waited patiently for their companion to speak. Having already experienced detachment, the decision to do it again voluntarily for the sake of a normal human would have been bad enough. But becoming the life-partner of a demon, especially such a powerful one, was almost asking the impossible — if it could even be done.

So many things could go wrong. Detaching alone was traumatic. Then there was the Shadow Demon, always lurking in the background, searching for detached *Les Gris*.

I have no choice. To refuse would be disastrous and I would be responsible.

No one would fault you for refusing, Ray. Few have survived what you have and stayed stable, Lighthra stated, giving her *Les Gris* partner a mental hug. *I've always admired your strength.*

We'll help you, Lunara promised, easing into the conversation. *Les Gris will protect you through your journey and stay with you until you stabilize. Longer, if you want.*

IF I stabilize! We know nothing about demons except the stories our people tell. What happens if this demon and I can't balance? You say you'll stay with me but how do you know you'll be able to? Demons aren't of this world and I'll be trapped in hers once I transition. Can you guarantee me that you'll be able to help me then?

Lunara hadn't thought about that and realized she couldn't. Although *Les Gris* were well aware that demons often wandered the mortal world, and occasionally came in contact with them, they had no desire to interact with them or their *Les Gris*. Apparently the feeling was mutual. Then again, perhaps neither had tried hard enough to communicate.

No, we can't, Lunara replied, honestly. *It was unfair of us to ask you to do this. Forgive us.*

"Yes," Belle agreed. "We'll just have to think of something else."

There isn't anything else, Lighthra interjected. *The decision must be yours, Raylena. You are the last hope. I know it's unfair to ask this of you. No one will fault you if you refuse.*

What would you do, Lighthra?

I don't know. I would want to do what is right and hope that I had that strength. Lighthra gave a mental shake of her head. *But, this isn't about me, is it?*

No. I almost wish it were. As you've said, there is only one choice. When do we begin?

In three days, the Blood Moon will rise. It will be an L5, the strongest possible umbral eclipse in several hundred years. It's our one shot at the merger.

And what makes you think the Child will agree to this?

Before anyone could answer, the air shimmered to Belle's left. Although she couldn't see, she felt the heat radiating near her and moved aside. Randi, who had been listening to the exchanges between the others, also felt the heat and turned to stare at the spot.

The three *Les Gris* watched the prism of light flickering, its colors as brilliant as starbursts and yet invisible to the human eye. From within its center two forms emerged from an oval portal. The portal snapped shut, but not before the Shadows caught a glimpse of the world beyond. Red and orange flames blazed brilliantly against the shadowy backdrop of a silvery blue sky, creating a breathtaking view of the Underworld. Startled, Randi jumped to her feet.

"She'll agree," the woman answered, her voice warm and husky.

"Or I will deal with her," the huge male replied. The deep baritone voice left no doubt that he meant business. "Already, I'm beginning to regret releasing her from the Netherworld. She's starting to test my patience."

"Wow!" Randi exclaimed, retreating a few steps backward. Realizing she had abandoned Belle, she side-stepped forward, grabbed the woman by the arm and pulled her a safe distance away from the intruders.

"What the hell?" Belle grumbled, slapping at the hand holding her.

"Ummm, I'm not sure you should be swearing like that," Randi whispered and then glanced at the giant standing a few feet away. Tall and muscular with dark red skin, he would have been impressive enough without the two horns protruding from his forehead or the hoofed feet. The leather jeans and vest did nothing to alleviate Randi's nervousness, although she found it almost comical that a demon would wear such human attire.

Raising both eyebrows, the demon crossed his arms and stared blandly at the human female. Biceps bulged even though he seemed relaxed.

"Would someone tell me what just happened?" Belle asked, irritated that Lunara was no longer sending her visual impressions.

Sorry, Lunara said and then projected an image of the two demons. Although it was distorted by the colors of light that normally accompanied the transmissions, Belle was impressed by what she was now seeing.

"I didn't hear you knock," she said amiably.

The comment was so unexpected everyone laughed — everyone but the male demon. Only the slight upward turn of his lips gave away his amusement. Bending slightly at the waist, he leaned forward, stared into the eyes of the blind woman and liked what he saw.

"You aren't afraid of me."

"Should I be?"

"If you are wise," Dis replied, making his voice slightly threatening to see how she would react.

"Oh, well then, I guess that explains it. I've never claimed to be wise."

Fascinated by the Underlord's unusual behavior, Lilith stood quietly watching. When Randi started to step forward, wanting to defend her friend, the demoness shook her head, warning the human not to intrude.

"I can give you your sight back," Dis offered out of the blue.

"At what price?" Belle asked, cocking her head slightly. The offer had taken her by surprise but she refused to give him the satisfaction of showing it.

Dis chuckled.

"Must there be a price?"

It was Belle's turn to laugh.

This is the person that instills such fear in humans? Lunara asked in amusement. *He appears quite civilized.*

He is playing with her, Lighthra interjected.

Maybe so. Still, I think he's kind of cute — in a demonic sort of way.

Trying to ignore the conversation, Belle held her ground, even though it seemed absurd to be having such a conversation with the most powerful demon known to mankind.

"If you're who I think you are, yes," she continued.

Straightening, Dis turned to Randi.

"You would defend this woman?" he demanded, letting her know he had seen her attempt to shield Belle.

Randi's mouth went dry and she swallowed.

"Ye...yes," she stammered and then stuck her chin out, daring him to challenge her.

Shaking his head, he turned to Lilith.

"I've been gone too long. No one fears me anymore," he grumbled and then winked so only she could see.

"So it would seem," she replied empathetically. "On the other hand, I believe these five beings are rather exceptional, so I wouldn't worry too much about it."

"Perhaps!" Turning back to Belle, he bent his knees and again stared into the blank eyes. "My offer stands with no price to pay. I can give you sight. Do you want to see again?"

Caught off guard, Belle hesitated. To see again had always been one of her greatest hopes.

Is this true? she asked Lunara.

Her *Les Gris*, who had been more interested in the actions of the demons, turned her attention back to her life-partner.

It's true. He can give you what you want.

And what about us? How will it affect us?

I don't know, Lunara lied. *We've been together a long time. Perhaps it will have no effect.*

Belle thought about all the years they had shared. Lunara was her light and her sanity. More important, she was her best friend. Sacrificing the bond between them for the ability to see seemed a huge price to pay.

Choose wisely, Lunara advised, knowing that if her life-partner were to regain her vision, Lunara would revert to the shadowy half-existence she had experienced when Belle had been able to see. *This is what you've dreamed of. Use your brain, not your heart.*

135

I'll use both. I think I'll pass on this one. Besides, having dreams gives me something to look forward to. Belle hadn't been fooled by Lunara's nonchalant attitude. Her life-partner's lack of emotion gave away the truth.

Stretching her hand upward, Belle moved it slowly in the direction of the warm breath fanning her face. As her fingers came in contact with Dis' cheek, he started to withdraw but then changed his mind. Had Belle been able to look into his eyes, she would have seen the flames of hell flaring brightly with amusement and curiosity.

Running her fingers gently across the surface of the demon's face, Belle developed a fairly accurate image of his features. The horns threw her off for a few seconds but then she chuckled.

"Is this the real you or a projection based on our legends?"

"Legends are based on reality, young woman. I can assure you these are quite real."

"I am going to turn down your kind offer," Belle said.

"That is your choice to make."

Straightening up, Dis glanced at Randi and then at the Shadows hovering around the well-lit room. "Do they speak?"

"Only to us and each other," Belle replied, sensing to whom he was referring.

"Can they communicate with us at all?"

No, Lunara answered.

"No," Belle translated.

"That's too bad. I'd have liked to learn more about them. Can they talk to my Shadow?"

We don't know.

"They don't know."

"Why? Is there something wrong with them?"

"If you mean our *Les Gris,* no. Yours may be a different story. Perhaps they aren't as evolved as human Shadows."

Dis snorted at the absurdity of the statement.

"Ridiculous! More likely they don't want to associate with primitives."

Realizing this could escalate into something confrontational, Lilith decided to step in.

"Be nice, Dis! Now isn't the time to debate superiority."

"You're right, of course," Dis replied. "Not that there is anything to debate. At the moment, though, I have guests waiting for me. Perhaps I should leave this matter for you to handle, Lilly. You were always better at dealing with humans."

Before she could reply, Dis vanished.

"Isn't that just like a male demon?" she asked and then turned to the others. "Tell me what I need to do."

Lunara quickly explained her plan to Belle, who passed the information on to Lilith.

"Lunara says it's imperative that the Child be ready for the merging before the Blood Moon rises. If she's even one second late, there's nothing we can do."

"She'll be there," Lilith promised.

"One more thing. *Les Gris* fear something called the Shadow Demon. They're afraid it might try to capture Raylena during the merger."

"This isn't a demon. I would know about it. I'm not sure what I can do to help other than to make sure Caelene isn't distracted."

Before anyone could reply, a black void opened near the kitchen door. Stepping from the darkness, Intunecat walked into the room.

Randi's mouth fell open and then she plopped down onto a chair, unable to speak.

"Good evening, Belle. Lilith, it's good to see you again."

"You too, Intunecat. You just missed Dis."

"Ah, too bad. I was looking forward to meeting him."

Lilith laughed. Having two powerful males in the same room would indeed have been interesting.

"Perhaps another time," he said and then turned to Randi. "I take it you are the human Belle mentioned?"

"Umm...yeah." Randi was at a loss for words. The whole evening was becoming too surreal.

"Has your *Les Gris* agreed to the proposition? We have a great deal to do in a short time."

I will do it!

"She's agreed to do it!" Randi translated.

"And Caelene?" Intunecat asked, looking at Lilith.

"My daughter has no choice."

"Unfortunately, she does," Belle interjected. "If she doesn't cooperate, it will never happen."

"Like I said, she has no choice."

"Then I guess there's nothing left to do but determine how we're going to do this," Belle said. "My biggest concern is protecting Raylena and the Child. And the *Les Gris* will be extremely vulnerable while they're focusing their energies on the joining."

"I'll do what I can to help," Intunecat offered, "but I'm not sure it will be enough. This Shadow Demon appears to be extremely elusive, otherwise I would have noticed it sooner."

"I'll provide demons to help you search the darkness," Lilith added. "Maybe between all of us, we'll scare it off or at least discover it before it does any damage."

It won't be enough, Lunara said. *As Intunecat pointed out, this demon is elusive. We need the Elementals to search the darkness. Hopefully Rainbow will be able to talk them into it.*

"Lunara doesn't think it will be enough," Belle explained. "She's hoping the Elementals will get involved."

"It's been a long time since I've heard them spoken of," Intunecat said. "Most have disappeared from this world, thanks to humans. Why would they agree now?"

"Lunara thinks they might. She's sent someone to ask them. If Rainbow can get the Aurora to help, we might just pull this off," Belle said.

"There is no *might,*" Lilith replied. "Failure isn't an option. I must be going now. I need to talk to Caelene."

If Belle could have seen Randi's face she would have laughed at the stunned expression as the demoness vanished. Without saying anything, Intunecat also disappeared, wanting to get back to his own realm. He had plenty to do and saw no reason to hang around once Lilith was gone.

"She...they..." sputtered Randi. "Did you see...I mean, of course, you didn't...but..."

Frowning, Belle turned in the direction of Randi's voice.

"Are you alright?"

She's fine, Lunara interjected, sending Belle an image of what happened. *Lilith's and Intunecat's sudden departure caught her by surprise.*

Oh! Is that all? Belle replied, unfazed. *Considering who they are, what did she expect? Besides, I'm finding it harder and harder to be surprised by anything anymore.*

I know what you mean. Meeting Lilith and Intunecat was impressive enough without Dis showing up.

He was rather interesting, wasn't he? I wish I could have seen him. Belle sighed dramatically.

You should have taken his offer.

Naw, I like things the way they are. Besides, he could never live up to my imagination, could he? Belle asked.

No, Lunara lied. Belle had sacrificed so much by refusing Dis' offer. Lunara felt guilty. The last thing she wanted was for Belle to think she had missed seeing someone as magnificent as him. *You'd have been very disappointed. Now I think you need to attend to Randi. Lighthra and Raylena are having a hard time calming her down.*

I can imagine.

"So Randi, how about some more homemade spaghetti?" Belle asked, moving toward her friend. Mumbling to herself, Randi just shook her head and followed the blind woman into the kitchen.

CHAPTER 21

The Elementals

RIDING AMONG the winds, the Sylph Wandra watched the leaves caught up in her wake scatter across the land. Nothing could stop her progress as she sped over the lands and seas, enjoying the freedom that only an air Elemental could experience. Occasionally, she would encounter another Sylph and they would frolic with wild abandon, catching the tumultuous gusts of winds that the summer thunderstorms kicked up. Eventually, exhausted, they would bid each other farewell and continue on their lonely journey.

There were so few of her kind left. They were a dying breed, caught up in the destruction that humanity had wreaked upon the planet. In time, like many other mystical creatures, they too would pass beyond, leaving the world a poorer place.

Wandra threw back her head and laughed. It felt good to ride the wild winds. Storms were her favorite, providing unpredictable twists and turns, ups and downs, at exhilarating speeds. Only hours before, she had been resting in her cloud cave, high above the Himalayas, enjoying the cold gusts that bounced off the snowy peaks.

Singing softly, her siren-like voice scattered in all directions. It was carried on the jet stream and eventually lost amongst the booming thunderclaps of a tropical storm. Still, it remained audible to her own kind. A Sylph could hear another Sylph from anywhere on the planet.

Now, sailing over the Blue Ridge Mountains, she glanced toward the earth and saw fires racing across the coastal plains of Georgia.

Salamanders, she thought and grimaced. *One of these days they're going to realize that even they are doomed if they don't stop their destruction.*

Changing direction to get a better view, she saw two Gnomes, a few miles north of the advancing flames, motioning for her to come closer.

Are you in trouble, my friends? she called out, hovering over the thermo-drafts the hot flames were causing as they heated up the air.

No, no, Cousin. We've been looking for you. Rainbow asked us to give you a message if we saw you.

And what message would that be?

She needs to see you. It's very important.

It must be for you to come so close to the Salamander's havoc. Thank you. Hurry now, the fires come. Have you a place of safety?

Yes, there's a cave nearby. It will provide safe harbor if we can beat the fires.

Hurry then! I'll send the winds to keep them at bay until you find shelter.

Thank you, Cousin, the *Gnomes* replied simultaneously. Waving goodbye, they set off toward a cavern, knowing the cool air would shelter them from the heat of the devastation.

Nodding her head, Wandra watched the two Gnomes until they disappeared into the darkness and then set out in search of Rainbow. It wasn't long before she found the colorful Boreal dancing above a storm blowing across the Atlantic waters, her shimmering body glistening in the sunlight.

Good morning, Sister. I hear you are looking for me.

Wandra, how are you? Rainbow yelled, making sure she could be heard above the roar of the thunder. In her excitement, she danced happily around the Sylph, her colors flashing rapidly.

I'm fine. Just caught a jet stream from the Arctic. It was quite refreshing. How are you?

Oh, quite well, thank you. It's a glorious day. The sun is so bright up here, I feel young again.

Wandra grinned. It was good to see her friend happy. The world of the Elementals was shrinking and many now lived in despair.

It's good to see you so full of life, but I hear you needed to talk with me.

Yes, I need your help...or at least my friend does. She's in a lot of trouble.

I'm sorry to hear that. What can I do?

I need you to take a message to the Aurora. They might be able to help her.

Who is this friend?

She is Les Gris.

Les Gris? Wandra asked in surprise.

Yes! It's a rather complicated situation. Perhaps I should explain what has happened.

Perhaps you should, the Sylph agreed.

Wandra knew that Rainbow had a special relationship with a few humans, unlike many of the Boreal. Although she, herself, held no animosity toward mankind, the Sylph wasn't exactly thrilled to assist them in any way, even if it was indirectly through one of their life-partners. After listening to Rainbow's story, she unconsciously shook her head, unsure of her feelings.

143

You know I never involve myself in human affairs, she said.

Yes, but this isn't just about them. It's about all of us. I fear our world will suffer greatly if we ignore their problem. A powerful demoness has lost her life-partner. Without her Les Gris, she'll eventually become unbalanced.

History is filled with unbalanced demons. What makes this one so different?

Rainbow danced nervously around Wandra, her brilliant blues and reds pulsating almost hypnotically.

She's the offspring of the Underlord and Lilith. Her potential for destruction is unimaginable.

Wandra frowned. Although the Elementals paid little heed to demons, they were very much aware of the damage demons had wrought upon mankind. Much of humanity's problems were rooted in the demons' penchant for creating trouble amongst believers. Interestingly, the non-believers were relatively safe from the mischief-makers. It was extremely difficult trying to get someone to see something they didn't think existed.

That could indeed be a problem. What can the Aurora do?

Les Gris need them to watch for the Shadow Demon while they try to bond another life-partner to this demoness. The transition has to take place during the Blood Moon.

Why can't they watch out? There are plenty of Les Gris to stand guard, Wandra said.

Their energies will be focused on the bonding. It will mean the humans and Les Gris are going to be vulnerable to an attack should it come. The Aurora may be able distract the Shadow Demon long enough for them to complete their task, Rainbow explained patiently.

If they're willing to help, you mean, which is a big 'if.'

You must convince them, Wandra. I can't stress the importance of this. There's no place this demon child can't reach if she wishes. Even the Aurora wouldn't be able to hide from her.

True, Wandra agreed. There were few places a demon couldn't access. *I'll try but I make no promises.*

That's all I can ask. Thank you.

Before departing, Rainbow gave the Sylph a more detailed plan of what needed to be done.

Call to me once you have an answer. I'll be as close as the daylight will allow me.

Good. Wish me luck.

Before Rainbow could respond, Wandra was whisked away on a strong gust of wind. Within minutes she disappeared into the mouth of a cave several miles away.

* * *

Several Aurora were gathered in a chamber amongst the crystal chandeliers of their dark subterranean home. Except for the constant dripping of water and occasional breezes sweeping through the labyrinth of shafts, the black world of these Elementals was quiet and peaceful. The heart of the earth provided them the one thing the surface could not...complete security. Even though humans had made great advances probing into the depths of these caverns, it would be a long time before they could reach the dark sanctuaries of the Aurora...perhaps they never would, and never suited the Elementals just fine.

Of course, the reclusive Elementals had one weapon against which even the humans couldn't defend, although they rarely used it. Should the intruders get too close to their homes, the Aurora could collapse entire cave systems, either trapping or blocking the uninvited visitors.

Aurora were different from other Elementals in that they loved to socialize. At any given time, there could be dozens of them packed together in the same cavern, gossiping about their newest exploits or openly copulating with any willing to partake in their favorite diversion.

Although they lived in darkness, they were quite capable of seeing everything around them. Nothing escaped their keen eyesight or sharp hearing, which gave them an advantage over everything entering their world. Wandra's arrival was no surprise.

* * *

"What brings you here, Sylph?" an invisible voice called out from the darkness.

"Forgive the intrusion, but it's imperative that I speak to your council."

"I speak for my people. Again I ask, what brings you here?"

Wandra could feel movement around her as the other Aurora stopped their playful antics to listen to the intruder. Sylphs were known for their sexual prowess and thus were the object of many a fantasy among the dark Elementals.

"I've come to deliver a message to you."

"And you are?"

"Wandra."

"Ah, well now, we're most honored to have you visit us. You're legendary among my people. It's said that you can satisfy even the lustiest of the Aurora."

Wandra would have denied it...if it weren't true. The fact was that she had enjoyed many sexual encounters with the different races of Elementals and was more than capable of fulfilling their wildest fantasies.

"There is truth in that," she replied matter-of-factly, "but that isn't why I'm here."

"That's too bad. I was looking forward to a little excitement. Perhaps another time."

"Perhaps," she agreed. "I've come as a messenger of the Boreal. They're in need of your assistance."

"It must be very important indeed. Our cousins rarely make such requests since our worlds are such opposites. We can only meet during the dawns and dusks. What can we do for them?"

"They need you to assist *Les Gris* in a ritual during the next Blood Moon."

"A ritual? Since when did *Les Gris* ever need help from Elementals? I've met a few over the centuries. They're a strange species, somewhat solitary considering their relationship to mortals."

"I suppose. It can't be pleasant knowing your very existence is so dependent upon another. We Elementals are lucky. We need no one to survive."

The Aurora laughed.

"Maybe you don't, but my people thrive on social interaction. Where there is one, there will be many. We're digressing though. I heard that a few *Les Gris* have become friends with some of the Sylph and Boreal but I've never heard of them requesting assistance before."

"Then you will understand their desperation. They don't make such requests lightly. Do you have a name?" Wandra asked. It felt odd talking to someone she couldn't see.

"Forgive my rudeness. I am Obsidia, descendent of Ebonia, Piceous and Negriscent."

147

From the tone, Wandra knew it was meant to impress her. Unlike most races of Elementals, it took three Aurora to create an offspring and the timing of their climaxes had to be perfect. Added to the problem was that each Aurora, who was hermaphroditic, had to adjust their gender at the moment of copulation to accommodate the other participants. This made success extremely difficult and reproduction rare. Only seven new Aurora had been conceived in the last eight hundred years. Fifty had disappeared without a trace, their numbers dwindling to only a few thousand.

They too were a dying race. As humanity's technologies grew, the ability to light the world had improved tremendously. Although the Aurora knew there were places mankind could never touch, deep within the bowels of Earth, they still felt the pressure of encroachment. Many resented humans. Others simply accepted their fate. A few, though, believed that in time Gaia would exert her will and bring the Earth back in balance and humanity under control.

"Tell me, Sylph, why should we help *Les Gris*? They mean nothing to us."

"Maybe not, but this is about more than just them. It's about all of us. You're old enough to remember what happened the last time a demon went berserk. Over twenty-one hundred square kilometers were leveled around the Tunguska River. We lost three Sylphs that day and over fifty of our cousins, including eighteen of your people."

Obsidia nodded. It was a day of sorrow for all of the Elementals. Not even the Salamanders in the area had been spared when the demoness Agra had slammed Sanarixs into the earth, furious because he had stolen souls that belonged to her. Only Dis' unexpected intervention had saved the demon from total destruction.

"Yes," he replied, remembering the helpless anger he had felt after discovering that Negriscent had been destroyed in the explosion. "This demoness, the one called the Child...you say she is more powerful than the others?"

"She's more powerful than hundreds of demons, maybe even thousands."

"Then we have no choice. Tell your friend we'll do what we can."

Wandra sighed in relief. Obsidia was a reasonable leader. Turning to leave, she felt something touch her shoulder.

"Surely your message can wait a little while," Obsidia suggested, his cool breath fanning her cheek as she looked behind her.

Never one to pass up a good time, the Sylph smiled.

"I don't think a few hours' delay will cause any harm. Will it be just you and I or are others to be invited?"

"I'll leave that decision to you," Obsidia replied unselfishly. Although it would boost his standing among his people if he could have Wandra to himself, he was always willing to share pleasure.

Realizing the sacrifice he was making, Wandra was impressed at his generosity.

"I think this time it will be you and I. The others I'll save for later. Come Obsidia, let me show you what it's like to be loved by a Sylph." And as she did, Obsidia knew that he would never again be completely satiated by his own kind.

CHAPTER 22

The Offer

CANDESCA WAS AWARE that the entity was gone. Hoping it would return soon, she decided to continue her search for others willing to join her cause. It was only a matter of time before she had a large enough following to force the Shadow Demon to release them. There was one thing that worried her, though. What would the freed *Les Gris* do then? Obviously, most wouldn't be able to rejoin their life-partners. Perhaps none of them would. Could they exist independently?

"They have no choice," she said to herself. "I did it for thousands of years. I can show them how."

Deciding now wasn't the time to worry about something that was probably a long way off, she moved through the darkness, recruiting those brave enough to incur the wrath of their captor. They were few in numbers but strong in their determination to escape the prison that held them. Candesca had no doubt that others would eventually gather their courage too.

* * *

It seethed, knowing that something needed to be done quickly. Summoning Rumex, the Shadow Demon ordered him to bring Candesca to him. Although his servant disappeared quickly, moments passed before both of them reappeared. Such behavior was unheard of and unacceptable.

"You are trying my patience," It hissed.

When Rumex was about to apologize, Candesca nudged him.

"Now's as good a time to choose as any," she advised. "As I've said before, It can't do any more to you than It has already."

"Fool!" It yelled angrily. "I can send all of you into oblivion if I choose."

"And then what? As far as I'm concerned, oblivion is a better place than here. At least we would be free of this place."

Now was It's chance! Seizing the moment, the Shadow Demon decided to change tactics.

"Free! Is that all you want? Why didn't you say so? You're free to go now," It declared magnanimously. "And you, Rumex! By all means, go! You've served me well."

Rumex gasped! Freedom! Could it be true? He had craved it for so long.

"Is it true?" he asked, turning to Candesca for confirmation.

"No doubt It's offer is real but is it really what you want? You will be alone once you've left this place. Will you be able to stand that?"

Alone! Hesitantly, he nodded.

"Then go, Rumex," Candesca said. "You are only one of what will be many. Eventually this *thing* will have to let all of us go. Perhaps we'll meet you on the other side."

"Aren't you coming?"

"No, that's what It's hoping for. I think I'll stick around for a while. The others need a leader. For the moment, I'm it."

"The offer only applies if you go, too," It growled. "It's both of you or neither of you."

Without answering, Rumex vanished, angering the Shadow Demon more. The terrified *Les Gris* had made his decision.

"I guess we'll be seeing you," Candesca pronounced and then disappeared, leaving a livid captor behind. Little did either of the *Les Gris* know that their decision would have a profound effect on the mortal world.

CHAPTER 2 3

The Gathering

THE FULL MOON was exceptionally bright, illuminating the darkness and casting shadows across the isolated beach. Belle and the other members of The Society had arrived earlier in the day after driving five hours to the secluded spot in the state park. Fortunately, a member of a sister group was a park ranger, so gaining access after closing hours wasn't a problem.

Shortly after sunset, Intunecat arrived. After greeting each human and their *Les Gris*, he wandered down the beach and into the nearby woods, checking for signs of intruders. No one but the invited must be present for the event.

"He still makes me nervous," Randi whispered.

Mallory was sitting on a dune with Ridge, her collie, staring out at the moonbeams reflecting off the ocean. The bond between the woman, the dog and their *Les Gris* was strong, making the four special. No one had protested when Mallory mentioned bringing Ridge, especially when Solly, her *Les Gris*, had suggested the collie could ward off any animals that might accidentally stray onto the beach while they were there.

Sylvie had convinced Angie to come along. Even though she wasn't sure she believed her partner's story, she couldn't shake the feeling that she needed to be there *just in case.*

Lumiere and Soleil were enjoying each other's company behind their life-partners' backs. The moon was bright enough to give them that rare moment when they could touch in the darkness. For them it was magical.

Thomas stood a slight distance away from the others, staring at nothing, his hands pushed deep into his pockets.

Why do I have to be here? he thought.

We are a part of them now, Beamon replied. *They need us.*

They need you, not me.

I couldn't help them if we weren't a team. Listen, Thomas. It's time you became the man you should be and not the one you were born to be. You must now decide our future.

Thomas looked at the others standing nearby. What did he have to lose?

* * *

Belle and Lunara were going over their plans again. Rainbow had appeared the day before to let them know that the Aurora had agreed to help but wouldn't be able to show up until the eclipse began. A full moon would weaken them some, so they didn't want to waste any energy waiting.

No one had heard from Lilith or the Child.

"Do you think she'll show up?" Belle asked her *Les Gris.*

I believe Lilith. She has no choice.

"I wish I was as confident. How is Raylena doing?"

She's nervous and, I think, frightened, but she's a survivor. She'll do what needs to be done.

Belle nodded. "I know. I guess we've done all we can."

Yes, now we wait.

* * *

Intunecat could feel the Aurora as they slid from amongst the trees and glided silently toward the group. Other than the faint darkening of the sand, nothing gave away their presence or their numbers. Hundreds of them poured unnoticed onto the beach.

Interesting, he thought. *I never realized so many still existed.*

* * *

Seeing Intunecat returning, Belle called the others together, unaware that the Elementals had surrounded them, establishing a barrier of Aurora so thick, nothing could sneak through their defense.

"Where's Caelene?" Randi asked, looking at Intunecat for an answer.

"She'll be here."

Looking at the sky, Randi fidgeted nervously. Raylena hadn't spoken to her or Lighthra all day. Already, they missed her presence.

As if on cue, the air shimmered near the small gathering, causing the Aurora to move aside. From within a portal, three figures emerged, causing a few gasps and some sighs of relief. Lumiere and Soleil chuckled at Angie's reaction, only to be reprimanded by Lunara.

Well, at least she believes Sylvie now, Soleil retorted, feeling the need to defend herself.

"Let's get this over with," Dis announced. "I have guests to attend to." Seeing the dark, hooded figure standing several feet away, he straightened to his full height and puffed out his chest.

155

"So, you are Intunecat. You're shorter than I imagined," he declared.

"Perhaps you're lacking in imagination, then," Intunecat replied, eyeing the demon with interest. The Underlord was impressive but his size didn't faze the dark spirit.

"Behave, Dis," Lilith warned, slapping his belly with the back of her hand. Giving her a rakish grin, Dis moved away and walked up to Belle.

"So, have you changed your mind yet?"

"No. I've decided I'm quite happy."

"Well, if you ever..."

"I won't!"

Laughing, Dis returned to Lilith's side and then turned to his daughter, who was unnaturally quiet.

"Are you ready?" he demanded.

"Do I have a choice?" she answered sullenly, remembering their last conversation. After throwing a temper tantrum and refusing to cooperate, she had mistakenly assumed the matter was closed and started to walk away. It wasn't! An invisible hand gripped her shoulders, forcing her to stop and then turn around. Fighting to break free, she eventually realized she was too weak to resist Dis' control over her.

"Never disrespect me again, Daughter," he warned solemnly. "I don't allow that from my followers and I won't allow it from you. Do you understand?"

For the first time in her life, she did. Even she did not have the power to control others like he had just demonstrated. After this was over with, she'd have to re-evaluate her plans to overthrow her father. That is *if* the humans' plan worked. Caelene could feel the tentacles of madness slowly creeping through her mind. Her thoughts were growing erratic, making it impossible for her to concentrate.

"I apologize, Sire," she said meekly.

"As you should."

That had been two days ago. The moment she had dreaded was here.

"I said, are you ready?"

"Yes, Sire."

"Let's get this over with," she added.

* * *

Lilith, who was standing by quietly, snapped her fingers, startling everyone. Immediately, portals opened outside of the circle of Aurora, and demons scurried out, forming an outer circle, twenty bodies deep.

"This is getting a bit crowded," Sylvie observed, staring in awe at the creatures circling them. Some looked like the clichéd demons she had seen on television and in comic books while others were either strangely beautiful or horribly ugly and deformed.

* * *

Obsidia wasn't sure he liked having the demons so close to his people. Some of the inhabitants of the Underworld were fire-makers. If they chose to play with fire while the Aurora were present, it would destroy many of them.

They don't dare do anything without their Underlord's permission, Lunara promised, sensing Obsidia's nervousness.

Perhaps, he replied, *but no one has complete control of his people, even him. I don't like this. No one said anything about this many demons being here.*

Trust me, Obsidia. My people will protect you as you protect us.

Reluctantly, he relented.

157

* * *

"Quickly," Belle called out. "The eclipse is starting. We must begin now. Randi, take Caelene's hands and put them over your heart. You must place your own on each side of her head and whatever happens, you can't break contact until the eclipse begins to recede."

Hesitantly, Randi walked over to Caelene and clasped her hands. Bringing them to her chest, she placed them on her heart. Flattening her palms, Caelene felt the human's heart pounding rapidly. She had never experienced the sensation before and was so fascinated, she jerked when Randi cupped her face with her own hands.

Surprised at how hot the demoness' skin was, Randi wasn't sure she'd be able to maintain contact with it for the time needed to complete the exchange. Already, her palms and fingertips felt on fire. Staring into Caelene's eyes, she saw flames flickering brightly and wondered if it was a sign of her growing madness. Guessing her thoughts, Caelene smirked and then cooled her skin to a bearable temperature.

You humans are so weak, she thought.

As are you, Raylena replied, hearing the thought. Startled, Caelene wasn't sure what to think, and frowned.

Get used to it! If this works, we'll be together for a long time. I don't like it any more than you, but it's your only hope. Already you're barely able to control the madness.

Unconsciously nodding, The Child pressed her hands firmly against the woman's breasts. Insanity was only a few heartbeats away.

Looking upward, Belle motioned her Society members to hold hands.

"I must be able to see," Belle said. Immediately, *Les Gris* united their energy, giving Lunara's life-partner what she needed.

Intunecat moved outside of the circle, making himself the first line of defense. Interestingly, he chose to stand next to the dog Ridge, who was lying down next to a strange-looking creature with horns and hooves.

"Nybbas," Intunecat said, acknowledging the little demon.

Lilith decided to follow suit, leaving Dis to protect their daughter, should the Shadow Demon break through the barriers.

It's is out of our hands now, Lunara said to everyone. She knew that humans as well as *Les Gris* could hear her while they were joined. *They will do all that they can to shield us. We must begin.*

"Fuck!" Mallory exclaimed and broke the hand contact to point toward the southern sky. Flashes of lightning illuminated clouds rolling rapidly toward the eclipse. "If it covers the moon during the eclipse, we're screwed."

"There's nothing we can do about it. We need to take our chances," Belle replied. "What happens, happens."

Everyone closed their eyes except Belle. With Lunara's visual assistance she had to focus all of her attention on the Blood Moon eclipse until the joining was complete. The others needed to concentrate on keeping their links strong. It only took one to break the chain and ruin everything. The sound of thunder rumbling in the distance made them jerk.

"Hold strong," Belle ordered, raising her voice slightly.

* * *

Leaving Nybbas and Ridge, Intunecat walked over to Obsidia.

"Can you not do something about the storm?"

"We are Aurora, not Sylph. Only they can control the winds."

"Is there a way to call the Sylph?"

Obsidia shook his head.

"If we're lucky, one will sense the storm and come to investigate. They love to ride the winds. The bigger the storm the better chance at least one will show up."

"Then we can only hope this one is huge."

* * *

Belle could see the storm closing in. One quarter of the moon was in shadow now. The *Les Gris* and their life-partners were beginning to weaken.

We were so worried about this Shadow Demon, we never considered that nature could ruin everything, Belle thought. *You're doing great, everyone. Hang in there.*

A bolt of lightning ripped across the sky, causing the Aurora to flinch painfully. It was rare, but if intense enough, lightning could harm or kill them. This one inflicted a few minor burns on several of them but they held their ground, scanning the darkness for signs of anything that seemed unnatural.

* * *

The moon was two-thirds covered. Randi was sweating profusely. She could feel Raylena being slowly drawn from her mind. The void left behind made her sick and disoriented. Legs trembling, she dared not fall.

Caelene felt the human's weakness and knew it was only a matter of time before the woman collapsed. Her new *Les Gris* was at the threshold of the crossover. Already, it was nudging the dark tentacles aside, searching for the void her own Les Gris had left behind. It was excruciatingly painful. The madness didn't give up its hold willingly. The battle for domination had begun.

* * *

Energy flowed from The Society members like a river gone wild. *Les Gris* and humans clung tightly to each other, feeding off of each other's strengths and using it to sustain the others. It was a race against time, and the clock was ticking. If the storm arrived before the ritual was complete, all their efforts would be in vain.

Violent gusts of wind whipped particles of sand into the air and launched them in every direction. Many of the small grains were blocked by the barricade of demons and then passed harmlessly through the Aurora. The humans, however, were less fortunate as the sand blasts pelted their faces and arms. It was like the stings of hundreds of tiny wasps, making it difficult for them and their *Les Gris* to concentrate.

We must stay strong! Lunara warned. *The joining is almost complete.*

Tightening their grips, everyone focused on their mission, knowing it was now or never.

* * *

The physical pain was excruciating but nothing like the hot daggers slicing through her brain. Randi tried her best to hold on but knew it was impossible. Tears streamed down her cheeks as she stared hopelessly into the fiery red eyes of the Child, begging her forgiveness. Caelene frowned, knowing there

161

was nothing she could do to help. Her own battle with the madness and the human *Les Gris'* alien composition was sapping all of her strength.

I can't help you!

I know!

Knees buckling, Randi's hands began to slip away from Caelene's cheeks. She had failed.

Sensing Randi's moment of weakness, Lilith realized she was too far away to help them. Within micro-seconds her daughter and the human would break their contact.

"Dis!" she screamed over the wailing winds and then realized her cry was wasted.

Watching his offspring and the human struggling against their inner demons and the elements, Dis knew they would never be able to fight both battles and win. Still, he wanted them to succeed on their own, knowing it would make both of them stronger. It was only at the final moment before they were to break contact that he intervened. An invisible force surrounded the two females, shielding them from the tiny particles assaulting their skin.

Randi, who had endured more than humanly possible, felt a burning energy flowing into her veins and muscles. Gasping, she tried to jerk her hands away from Caelene's face only to find it impossible to move them.

"You've come too far to fail now, human," Dis said matter-of-factly. "The joining will continue."

Without breaking her gaze with the demoness, Randi slowly nodded her head, signaling she was ready to continue.

* * *

Concentrating on the final stages of the eclipse, Belle saw a dark cloud stretching ahead of the others and moving rapidly toward the moon.

Could that be the Shadow Demon? she asked the *Les Gris*.

We're not sure! No one has ever seen it, they replied in unison. Belle and the others could feel their fear. The Aurora tightened their circle around the humans, pressing their shadowy shapes against each other to insure that the shadow would have no space to gain access to even one of them. Immediately the demons moved closer. Lilith and Intunecat watched the cloud as it stretched itself unnaturally toward the moonlight and then began circling it counter clockwise. Dis glanced up and then back at Randi and Caelene.

Everyone knew they had lost! The cloud would block out the Blood Moon's energy before the joining was complete.

"Is there nothing we can do?" Thomas yelled, finally understanding the importance of their mission. "We are so close! We can't give up now!"

Beamon was proud! For the first time in his life, Thomas had taken the initiative even if it was too late to save Raylena and the Child.

CHAPTER 2 4

It Returns

THE SHADOW DEMON was pissed! Storming through the darkness, It shoved the frightened *Les Gris* aside, searching for Rumex or Candesca. How dare they leave It's presence without permission!

In time, It realized that the realm was too big. They could be anywhere and it would take forever to find them if they chose to avoid the Shadow Demon. In creating the realm in Intunecat's dark world, It had brought into existence hiding places that were infinite.

Finally giving up, It decided to seek solace in the mortal world. Surely there were Shadows waiting to be had. They were the most vulnerable during the Blood Moon.

Yes, It thought. *Gather your puny forces. I'll replace them a thousand fold.*

Deep from within the realm of Darkness, It emerged, gleefully laughing. No one defied the Shadow Demon.

* * *

Emerging near the windswept beach, It watched the group standing silently in a circle. Several beer bottles and soda cans were strewn around them. The Shadow Demon was pleased. Alcohol and drugs weakened the bond between life-partners, making it easier to seduce a *Les Gris. Perhaps It would be able to add several to It's collection this night.*

The Blood Moon was in full eclipse although partially blocked by clouds. The timing was perfect. Gliding through the dark night, It found a weak *Les Gris* and his human sitting in the sand near the others.

You are unhappy, It said sympathetically. *Your life-partner doesn't deserve you.*

The *Les Gris* sighed. *We are joined. I have no choice.*

You do now. I can help you. Come with me and I will show you paradise.

Paradise?

Yes, a land of light and joy. Colors as you never imagined — and others like you who have chosen happiness. I'm offering you that!

Why? The *Les Gris* asked. *Who are you?*

Just another like you who has vowed to help my brethren.

The *Les Gris* felt a warmth creeping into him. He had longed for freedom from the wretched man who was his life-partner. Without hesitation, he embraced the warmth and was lost.

Joyously, the Shadow Demon laughed as It ripped the Shadow from his human. There would be more to follow once this one was ensnared within the darkness.

CHAPTER 2 5

The Joining

HELPLESSLY, THE gathering waited for the cloud to cover the Blood Moon. They had done all they could, but it wasn't enough. In less than ten minutes the joining would have been complete. With the cloud circling the eclipse it was only a matter of seconds before it...

Suddenly, the cloud stopped. In an unnatural maneuver, it turned toward the beach and streaked forward, twisting and swirling like a snake until it came to an abrupt stop in front of Obsidia.

Good evening, Cousin! Wandra frolicked within the swirling streams of cloud.

Wandra! It's good to see you, the Aurora declared happily. *You had us worried.*

Sorry about that! It took me awhile to figure out where you were. The rest of the Sylphs are in the storm. They will hold it at bay until the ritual is complete.

We are in your debt. Thank you, Cousin.

My pleasure! I will collect on that debt in a few days, Wandra promised. *If you are up to it.*

Obsidia vibrated ecstatically. His influence within the Aurora would grow even more once they knew he was to enjoy a second union with the Sylph.

I can think of nothing better to keep me fit, he replied. *I'll await your pleasure with anticipation.*

Nodding her head slightly, Wandra turned the cloud and rode it back into the heart of storm. Lightning flashed wildly while thunder rumbled. Although the winds raged, they held their position as an invisible force blocked their path.

* * *

Lunara and other *Les Gris* held firm as Raylena slipped from their grasp, disappearing into the mental maze of the demoness' mind. Like a springing trap, a black fiery portal snapped shut, blocking Raylena's energies. The joining was complete. Everyone had done all they could. It was now up to Caelene and Raylena to make the merging successful.

* * *

The Child collapsed to the ground, exhausted. Releasing Randi from his invisible grip, Dis watched her as she sank slowly to the ground. Satisfied that her weakness was only temporary, he looked around and grinned.

"I have a party to attend," he announced happily, and then he vanished. The demons quickly followed.

Without commenting, the Aurora faded into the dark woods. They too wanted to celebrate as only the Aurora could. The orgy would go on for weeks.

* * *

Lilith approached her daughter, helping both her and Randi to their feet. The Society members and their *Les Gris* gathered around them, wanting to make sure the two women were okay. They knew that both would need a good support system until they adjusted.

"We miss her already," Randi said, feeling a deep loneliness. Everyone assured her and Lighthra that it would pass.

I can still feel her presence, Lighthra said, overwhelmed with joy. *She says she's fine but a little lost. The Child's mind is so different. It will take them time to adapt to each other.*

But she's optimistic? Lunara asked.

Cautiously so. It will be hard for each of them. The Child's thoughts are...Raylena can't seem to come up with a good description. She says it's like a multi-dimensional maze. At the moment she is running into mostly dead ends but isn't giving up. Already the madness is receding.

Raylena is strong and will be a good match for the Child, said Lunara.

Everyone else agreed.

* * *

"Are you alright?" Lilith asked, leaning slightly forward to make eye contact with the human. Randi had risked her life to help Caelene... and more. The sacrifice could have cost the human more than she had bargained for.

The demoness wouldn't forget Randi's generosity.

Randi rubbed her aching temples and groaned.

"I think so," she replied hesitantly. "I could use a couple of aspirin right now."

"I have something better," Lilith said as she ran her fingertips across the woman's forehead.

"Wow!" Randi exclaimed as the pain subsided. "Thanks. I do feel better."

"Good." Lilith wrapped her right arm around her daughter's waist. "It's time to go home," she said. Giving Intunecat a faint nod, she and the Child disappeared as the Dark Spirit also vanished.

* * *

"He's not real accomplished with goodbyes, is he?" Mallory observed as she ruffled the fur around Ridge's neck. "It seems so anti-climactic now, doesn't it? All of these entities joining together to fight the big bad Shadow Demon and it doesn't even show up for its own party."

Are you disappointed? her Les Gris Solly asked.

"No. At least I don't think so. It would have been fun to see his expression, though."

His?

"Okay hers, then, although this sounds more like a guy thing to me."

Solly chuckled.

Said like a true human.

Mallory shrugged.

"Said like a true *Les Gris*. I guess we should get a move on. Tomorrow's another day and I still have those flowcharts to do."

Pulling a ball from her pocket, she threw it toward the car. Immediately Ridge charged after it. Mallory and Solly could almost imagine what he was thinking...*about time!*

* * *

169

"Let's go, everyone," Belle called out and motioned toward the parking lot. Swaying from fatigue, she wasn't aware that Thomas had stepped close to her until he took her by the arm.

"I can..."

Let him help you this time, Lunara advised. *It's his and Beamon's way of letting you know they have begun stabilizing.*

"Oh, alright," Belle grumbled under her breath. "Thank you, Thomas," she said graciously to the young man. Without thinking, Thomas gave her a shy smile. "The footing here is deplorable. You coming girls?" she called out to Sylvie and Angie.

"Naw," Angie said, smiling happily. "I think we'll stay a little longer. It's been quite a while since we had time to ourselves on an isolated beach."

"Yeah," Sylvie piped in. "Besides, with the full moon, I know of two *Les Gris* who are going to enjoy their first romantic interlude on the sand."

Giggling, Lumiere and Soleil didn't wait for their life-partners to begin. Embarrassed, Sylvie and Angie clasped hands and ran toward the lapping waves. Had Angie glanced behind them, she would have noticed their Shadows happily frolicking in the moonlight.

"We should go," Thomas said. "I...uh...think we should give those two women some privacy."

You mean Lumiere and Soleil, Beamon corrected and then decided to change the subject. Thomas was obviously embarrassed too. *You've done well, Thomas. Perhaps one day, you'll meet someone and know the same type of love.*

Beamon was proud of his life-partner. He now believed that in time they would be in sync. Then Beamon would take a much deserved rest, although he wasn't planning on going anywhere. How could he?

All in all, it had been an interesting experience for everyone.

EPILOGUE

INTUNECAT STUDIED the black orbs as they floated around him.

"One of these days, I'll learn your secret," he promised aloud. Although they were impossible to tell apart, he could identify one in particular. It always kept close to him, whereas the others maintained a safe distance. Occasionally, he would forget about it and then would suddenly become aware that it was resting lightly on his left shoulder.

In a way, he felt comforted and some of his loneliness was diminished. No matter who or what the orb was, Intunecat was sure it was intelligent and it was only a matter of time before he learned its secret.

* * *

Candesca felt an affinity to the entity near her. She had felt its return and rushed from her hiding place to join it. Sensing its loneliness, she remembered the years she had been alone waiting for her life-partner to reappear.

Although she had willingly chosen this new prison until she could free the other Shadows, it felt good to know she had a companion who enjoyed her presence. Already, she could interpret its moods. At the moment, it appeared calm on the surface but inside, a dark fire burned, much like that within the Child. The thought gave her comfort. She understood the heat of suppressed passion.

The End

LES GRIS PERSONNES

For the Animal Lovers

THEY WERE *Les Gris Personnes*, the Shadow People. At least that was what they liked to call themselves. Their past was as much a mystery to them as their future, which suited them fine. The present was what mattered...along with their life-partner, that is. This is the story of a bond between two souls whose very survival is dependent upon each other and one four-legged companion who perhaps understands them better than they do themselves.

Punching in a code, Mallory sat back as the data began to flash across the monitor.

"You really think this is the problem?" she murmured, ignoring the strange glances from her fellow consultant.

You always ask me that. Have I ever been wrong? Solly asked.

"Yes! Where would you like me to start?" Mallory continued as her gaze returned to the monitor in front of her.

Mallory snickered and then glared at the tech sitting a few feet away when he looked up questioningly. Tim quickly lowered his eyes and pounded furiously at the keyboard, mumbling under his breath.

Tim already thought she was nuts but was usually willing to overlook her peculiarities as long as she did her job — and Mallory always did her job.

That was four years ago and I wasn't wrong. I just wasn't entirely right, and you know it.

"In my book that makes you wrong, so quit sulking. I hate it when you sulk."

Les Gris don't sulk.

Mallory snorted and then glared at Tim again when he shifted uncomfortably on his chair.

"You have a problem?"

"Uh, no. I was just...well..." Looking around nervously, Timothy swallowed. Mallory was an excellent IT professional but her penchant for talking to herself was too freaky for him. Still, he refused to put in for a transfer since she made him look good. She made the whole team look good.

"You were just?" Mallory asked, swiveling her seat around to make eye contact.

"Geez, Mal, you know it freaks me out whenever you start that shit. I never know if you're talking to me or yourself. It's just not normal."

He's such a wuss!

Be nice, Solly!

I'm sorry. I didn't mean it like it sounded.

Mallory chuckled. Tim was a nice guy. Perhaps a little too sensitive for the career he had chosen but that wasn't any of her business.

"I know. I've told you to ignore me when I talk to myself. It's just my way of solving things."

"Yeah! I have to admit you're at your best then. Still..."

"Look Tim, I'm not changing who I am because it makes you uncomfortable. Get used to it or transfer out. Now, do you mind if I get back to work?"

Mallory felt her *Les Gris* give a mental shake of the head.

"And don't even think it," she muttered. "He's not the only one who thinks I'm nuts."

Which only goes to show you how right I am. Again!

"Oh be quiet and get to work. We have to figure this out by tomorrow or lose the contract."

"I'd be able to concentrate better if you'd talk a little less," Tim interjected, again thinking she was talking to him. Shaking his head, he decided that he was just going to ignore her from now on.

"Like I haven't said that a thousand times already," he grumped.

You really should be nicer to him. Sunnie says he's terrified of you.

"Sunnie needs to work on Tim's self-confidence then. Now, do you think we can get back to work? I need to get home and let Ridge out."

Alright! How about stopping the application server and restarting it to let it rebuild the cache? Then clear the browser cache and we can reconnect to the application.

Leaning close to the monitor, Mallory squinted, allowing her tired eyes time to adjust to the data in front of her.

"I just don't see it. What am I missing?"

Trust me! This should work and then we can go check on Ridge.

* * *

Mallory sat back and rubbed her eyes. Exhausted, she looked at her watch and realized it was too late to make it to the meeting. Sighing, she put her head on her folded arms and closed her eyes. The Society would have to do without her tonight. She only hoped nothing had happened to any of the members.

Belle had indicated that it was an important meeting and these were strange times. More and more life-partners were de-syncing. Some had even become separated from each other. The results from either scenario were catastrophic for both human and *Les Gris*. If they didn't find out soon what was going on, the problem could become epidemic.

It's only a meeting tonight. Belle and Lunara have things under control at the moment. They'll understand if we don't show up. You really should get those glasses. Putting it off isn't going to make the astigmatism go away.

"I don't need glasses. I'm just tired." Mallory hated being reminded of her deteriorating eyesight. It made her feel old.

After what you did to Benton's nephew, I'm not surprised. Neither of them is going to appreciate being humiliated like that.

"Like I give a rat's ass. If the young brat hadn't been so pompous, I'd have gone easy on him."

Thinking back to the moment she decided she disliked her client's nephew, Mallory grinned. The two men had arrived late in the morning to check on the progress of the team hired to resolve their company's software problems. At first she tried to ignore the arrogant young man as he ineptly explained to his uncle what Mallory was doing, and speculated on why she hadn't been able to bring the system back online sooner.

"It's really complicated, Uncle, but a good tech should have had everything working several hours ago. I wish you'd have just listened to me before you contracted with Einyxweb."

"I was told they were quite reputable, Herbert, but I'm beginning to wonder. Every minute we're down, we're losing money. I've a mind to bill Fred for our losses."

Grinding her teeth, Mallory glanced at Tim, who was doing his best to pretend he wasn't listening to the two intruders.

Sighing, Mallory pushed her chair back and turned to the pompous, fat balding man standing slightly behind her.

Be nice! He's the client!

"I know," Mallory grumbled. "Can I help you Mr. Benton?"

"You certainly can. Why the hell is it taking you two so long to fix that thing? My nephew here says it should have been fixed by now. I'd hate to think you're stalling to get more money from my company."

"Perhaps if I explain what we're having to do, you'll have a better picture of the complexity of the job," Mallory replied, fighting to contain her temper. Without waiting for an answer, she launched into the technical details of her job.

"The Production system was up and running about three hours during first shift. Third shift went smoothly and the rollover to Europe from Asia-Pacific went great. Europe was entering new cases as usual and all the cases were routed to the correct queues for evaluation and back-office processing, call-outs, and straight-through processing as appropriate.

We were business as usual until hour four. At that point Europe reported that all the cases entered during the beginning of their shift had vanished off the queues. Line Managers couldn't see them in their Management Dashboard reports and all the Trend Analysis and Real-Time reporting stats were skewed."

"I dug into the issue as the alert was a Stage 3 severity, and all hands were called in. Having accessed the database, I determined that all the cases were indeed in the database, but that the cases entered from hour four onward were in the NEW schema. The cases entered for the first three hours were in the old schema. I checked the cutover switch in the app and found the cutover date was set today...."

"That's not possible," Herbert piped in. "We're not scheduled to apply the new schema until the end of the month." He looked at his uncle, and continued contemptuously. "She's on the totally wrong track here. My Release Evaluation Committee approved that just this week. We've got ten days before the migration."

Mallory drew a deep breath and then resumed her explanation, hoping her impatience wouldn't be noticed.

You're beginning to enjoy this too much, Solly chided.

Not! Mallory shot back and then continued on, knowing her life-partner was right. If she played her cards right, she'd have the brat just where she wanted him before striking the final blow.

"As I was saying, I ran an extract of the database and can show you the cases from the first three hours if you'd like. We determined in the All Hands con call that the best course of action was to shut down until the cause of these issues could be determined. We tried conferencing you in, but um...I guess you were in a bad cell phone area."

Herbert shifted uncomfortably.

"I was at my desk. Why didn't you just call my desk phone? There are no messages on my PDA...you could have texted..."

Mallory interrupted, "Hmm. I hate to say this but we tried your desk. The receptionist paged you throughout the offices, and as a favor to me she tried not only your cell but also your home phone. Delores texted you and also sent email, which she copied to the Distribution List. Europe forced a decision and we had to proceed without you."

Mr. Benton broke in, "Herbert..."

Herbert opened his phone and hit a few buttons. Suddenly the thing vibrated to life, causing him to drop it. Picking it back up off the floor, Herbert said, "Uncle I keep begging IT for tools that work. I can't be blamed for their incompetence. Besides, we were discussing why Mallory hasn't resolved the Production Down. Mallory, stop changing the subject. Obviously you're just stalling for time."

I'm not stalling for time. You're wasting my time, you prick! Okay. Keep it together, Mallory thought. But she knew better than to voice it.

See, patience is a virtue. You're learning, Solly said, giving her a mental pat on the head.

"Quit that!" Mallory hissed. Herbert jumped and looked at his uncle who seemed taken aback by the outburst. Giving them both a fake smile, she continued on.

"I called the Network Operations Center, and got my friend Dave, the Executive NOC Director. We implemented a Level 1 Lockdown, rolled over the CTI and automated dialers, sent out an email, text, and phone blast to the Business and proceeded with triage."

"I got copies of all of that," Mr. Benton acknowledged. "That's why I'm here. Continue."

Mallory shifted her attention to him.

"Sir, as I said, the cutover to the new schema was set in the application for today's date and I checked the record for when hour four started. The data for the switch shows it was triggered manually. Now, that's the setting we were going to change at the end of the month as Herbert pointed out.

"I wrote a stored proc in the database and did a quick count. There are 47,016 cases in the old schema entered today. There were about 17K in the new schema and I was hoping we could get the 17K to convert back into the old format, but then the XML feed came over MQ from the self-service website. We had to let the feed finish before shutdown."

Mr. Benton nodded. So far he had been able to follow her description of events.

"At that point we had almost as many cases in the new schema as the old. We already got signed off on the dynamic upgrade from the old schema to the new, so we can expose the columns required for the new Trend Analysis and Data Mining Initiatives. I used that on the cases from first shift. Until all cases entered during first shift are in the same format, they won't process on the queues or show in the reports properly."

Feeling he was being left out, Herbert decided it was time to take back control of the situation.

"How hard can it be to upgrade 47,000 cases? This is an enterprise server we're talking about." He looked at his uncle to confirm he'd scored some points for that remark.

"Yes, and each of those 47,106 cases has at least four dependent objects that also have to be ported to the new schema. This is going to take some time. Tim's monitoring that now," Mallory explained.

"We're losing money by the minute. I'm calling Fred," said Benton.

Mallory summoned her patience once again. *Give me strength. Just a little bit longer.*

Solly decided not to comment on her life-partner's thoughts. Mallory had the situation pretty well under control, as well as her temper.

"I can't believe we were sent such incompetent consultants."

Herbert's interruption was the final straw. Annoyed, Mallory knew she had to stop this now or she'd end up slugging the arrogant bastard.

Go get him! Solly prompted, knowing her life-partner had suffered enough.

"Alright, that's it!" Mallory growled. "Look, I'm trying to fix the problem and if you..."

181

Cool it! Now isn't the time to blow your top! He'll get his just due if you handle this properly.

Mallory sighed.

"Mr. Benton, I'm doing what I was authorized to do at the All Hands meeting. We're on a time schedule here and I have to report to the others in less than thirty minutes."

"I was at the All Hands," Benton stated. "So how long is the script thing going to take?"

Herbert piped in, wanting to impress his uncle by asserting himself. "The system's down. How could this all happen? You're the expert. It's your system. Are you holding it together with duct tape and chewing gum?"

Mallory smiled. *Excellent question!* "The application is functioning to specifications. As I said, the cutover to the new schema was triggered manually today. I checked the user ID used and contacted Dave at the NOC. I was just – "

"Uncle, let's go back to your office and get this Dave on the phone. Maybe we can grab the CIO while we're at it. We'll get to the bottom of this. I've said all along we should make some changes around here."

Gotcha! Solly exclaimed enthusiastically.

"You bet your...ummm...As a matter of fact, Mr. Benton, I was on the phone with Dave when you walked in." She hit the mute button on her speaker phone and said, "Dave, you still there?"

There was a pause and then Dave's voice came over the speaker phone, "Yeah. I'm still here. Mute-itis strikes again eh, Mallory? You left me hanging."

"Sorry, Dave. Mr. Benton and Herbert are here. Would you share the information you have on our security breach?"

"We ran a reverse lookup on the user ID, Secure ID, and PIN used to alter the cutover setting and override the online lockout security measure. The ID belongs to Herbert O'Rourke.

Herbert, I've been trying to contact you. Since we had a security breach under your ID, Security Protocols went into effect. We locked out your Global Sign-on, cut off all systems access...and suspended your badge."

Benton looked at Herbert, who was beet red. Herbert almost came off the floor as he shouted, "That's NOT possible! I was supervising our user acceptance test for Release *3.1* today starting at 5:00 a.m. We kicked off the upgrade to test reporting first thing and..." He glared at the phone and then at Mallory.

Mr. Benton said, "Herbert, we'll finish this discussion in my office. Your ignorance has cost us at least several thousand dollars. Mallory, Dave, keep me posted on your progress. I want updates every thirty minutes until we're back up and running." He and Herbert turned and left the office. Tim and Mallory smiled at each other as they heard Herbert whining half-way down the hall.

Mallory picked up her headset and said, "Hey Dave, gonna let you go now..."

"Thanks. Back at ya in 30." He hung up.

Mallory took a deep cleansing breath.

Now wasn't that fun? Solly asked, giving Mallory a mental nudge. *You did well.*

"Thanks. Let's finish this up and get out of here."

RIDGE

Ridge was restless. Unable to endure his baleful looks, Mallory sighed and put down her laptop.

"Why do you always do this just when I'm settling in?" she asked, pointing her finger at the rough coated collie accusingly.

His cocked head and happy, toothy grin made her laugh. Ruffling his fur, she stood up and headed for the door. She slipped a leash into her pocket, although no leash was required. Ridge was the perfect gentleman when it came to their walks to the park.

"You realize you're taking me away from some important business?"

Ridge barked once and wagged his tail enthusiastically. He knew by her tone that his human didn't object to the distraction.

You realize he isn't fooled by your objections. He's got you pegged.

"Yeah, but I still have an image to uphold, Mallory replied.

Uh huh! You call catering to his demands upholding an image? What would Cesar Millan say about this?

The Dog Whisperer? He'd be quite impressed with how well behaved Ridge is and you know it.

Right!

The walk to the park took about twenty minutes. Although the weather was a little cool, the sun was bright and the skies clear. Long shadows stretched along the streets, indicating it would only be a few more hours until dusk.

Ridge walked patiently next to Mallory, his keen sense of smell and sight monitoring everything around him.

He enjoys these moments, Solly observed.

"Not as much as you, I imagine," Mallory replied, glancing at the long shadow preceding her. With the sun at her back, Solly's image was stretched far in front of her. "I know you don't get as much natural light as you'd like with the hours we put in on the job."

Giving a mental sigh, Solly agreed.

We all pay a price for living. Mine is small compared to others.

"Always the practical one eh?"

Not really, but I'm working on it. It hasn't always been this easy for us, has it?

"No," Mallory agreed, her mind wandering back a few years. "No, it hasn't."

As a child Mallory had always been fascinated with gadgets. Her parents couldn't keep her away from anything that had buttons or knobs. When she was five, they had bought her a Simon Says game. The brightly colored lights and tones mesmerized her. She would play with the game for hours trying to keep up with the different light patterns displayed. At first, her parents thought it was great. It kept her occupied and out of trouble.

Eventually, though, they recognized that something was seriously wrong with their daughter. Mallory refused to go anywhere without her toy. Finally, out of desperation, they took it away from her only to find she became unresponsive to everything else, including them.

"I don't see the harm in letting her have it back," her father had argued.

"It's just not natural," her mother, Cynthia, had replied. "I think she needs therapy."

"Therapy! She's five years old for Christ's sake. It's natural for her to want to play with toys. Hell, when I was young, I had my GI Joes and stuff. They went with me everywhere."

"That's different and you know it, Paul," Cynthia said. "Mallory's obsessed with this thing. I've never seen anything like it. And what about that imaginary friend of hers? She never mentioned this Solly person before she got that game."

Paul shook his head. It was true Mallory talked continually to herself now, as if Solly were real. Still...

"Listen, most kids have imaginary friends. This is just a phase. Let's give her awhile longer and see what happens."

Giving up, Cynthia shook her head in disgust, knowing in her heart something was definitely wrong with their only child. In time, though, it did appear that Paul was right. Mallory soon lost interest in Simon Says. The electronic age was no longer in its infancy and her addiction for gadgets grew. By then Paul and Cynthia decided that Mallory was just one of those children who would grow up to be a computer whiz. They were right but not for the reasons they thought.

It took me a long time to overcome my addiction, Solly admitted, following Mallory's thoughts. *I still want to examine everything new that's on the market.*

"I know. I feel the same way. I guess we'll never be over our electronics addiction but at least we can get our fix working in the computer field. These twelve-hour days pretty much tire me out to the point I don't even want to turn on the television when we get home."

Yes, and that's a blessing and a curse for me. I don't have the physical ability to manipulate things so I'm pretty much dependent on you that way.

"Does that bother you?" Mallory asked. She had never really considered that aspect of their relationship.

Sometimes, but not often. It helps me keep my cravings under control. In reality it's my addiction that makes us the way we are. You, unfortunately, suffer from the residual effects.

"Maybe. Still, we make a good team so I wouldn't change anything for the world," Mallory said and smiled. Lifting her hand, she watched her shadow as she patted the top of her head. "You're a good person."

I think you just freaked that guy out, Solly observed and quickly pointed to a man standing in his yard raking leaves.

Had anyone been watching Mallory's shadow, they would have been stunned to see it moving independently from the human's actual motion.

"You keep doing that and he really will be freaked out."

Solly laughed softly and then remembered a moment when she had accidentally startled Mallory's first serious friend.

At seventeen, Mallory knew she was attracted to girls. Being reclusive, though, she found it hard to socialize with others her age. Unfortunately, most of her classmates thought she was either weird or snobbish so they avoided her...all but one that is.

Kathy Grinley was short for her age. At barely five feet tall she was often teased by the rest of her class. For the most part, Kathy took their comments in stride, knowing it wouldn't accomplish anything if she objected. Perhaps it was because of her own experiences that she felt empathy for Mallory, then interest.

Unfortunately for Kathy, Mallory didn't feel the same way. At first, she did her best to ignore the freckle-faced kid who insisted on hanging around her. When that didn't work, she warned Kathy that her friends wouldn't like her associating with a weirdo. Kathy merely shrugged her thin shoulders and then smiled mischievously.

"That's okay. At least they might come up with a better nickname to call me. Shorty isn't very imaginative, you know?" Kathy quipped and grimaced.

Mallory had to agree.

"And I suppose *freak geek* sounds better to you?"

Works for me, Solly interjected.

"Hush!" Mallory grumbled.

"I didn't say anything," Kathy replied, giving her a strange look.

Mallory blushed. She and Solly were always bantering back and forth. Sometimes it was silently, but other times Mallory would forget herself and speak aloud. It was always embarrassing.

"I didn't mean you," she said and then realized how stupid that sounded. Kathy cocked her head slightly and waited for an explanation. Sighing, Mallory knew she needed to say something. "I talk to myself. It's a bad habit but I can't help it."

"You mean like Tourette's?" Kathy teased, knowing better.

Mallory snorted.

"Not hardly!"

She's funny, Solly observed. *Too bad she and her Les Gris grew apart. They'd have had fun together.*

Mallory nodded her head. She had known for a long time that most people lost conscious contact with their life-partners. Sadly it was an almost inevitable result of growing up. With maturity came the realization that childhood *friends* were only the products of overactive imaginations.

Go ahead and take a chance, Solly advised. *She's got a good heart and she likes you. You two will be good for each other.*

Solly had been right. For the next three years, they had been almost inseparable. Needless to say, rumors abounded about them being lesbians and eventually progressed to the expected conclusion that they had to be lovers. Neither Mallory nor Kathy minded. After all, sometimes the truth didn't hurt.

It was during their third year of college that tragedy struck. Kathy and Mallory were driving back to the dorm in Kathy's Spyder convertible. The two young women were chattering away about the upcoming Easter break. Neither saw the fat little squirrel dart onto the road until it was too late. Without thinking Kathy jerked the wheel to the right causing the car to spin out of control.

Before either realized what had happened, the vehicle slammed into a pole, causing the airbags to deploy. Kathy was knocked out for a few minutes when her head slammed sideways into the driver's side window. Mallory, who had braced herself, was shaken but unharmed. Struggling to release her seatbelt, she cursed loudly.

She's okay, Mallory. Calm down, Solly advised.

Before Mallory could reply, Kathy groaned and slowly opened her eyes, only to snap them closed again.

"Hey, kiddo, you okay?" Mallory asked, reaching over to brush the bangs from Kathy's forehead as she stared at her friend with concern.

"No... I mean, yes. I think. What happened?"

"Some fuckin' squirrel tried to kill us. I hope we ran over him."

Oh you do not! Quit being so dramatic! Solly admonished.

"You call almost getting killed dramatic?" Mallory demanded, her voice raised in anger.

"Hey," Kathy whispered. "It was an accident! The important thing is we're okay."

Mallory grinned sheepishly.

"Sorry. I wasn't really talking to you."

"Oh, okay. Your Solly, I take it." Mallory had told her a little about her life-partner. While Kathy never believed Solly was real, she understood that Mallory needed her *imaginary friend* as an outlet for her frustrations.

Opening her eyes, Kathy blinked several times trying to focus on her friend's face. The bright afternoon sun was painfully bright. It was only when a shadowy hand passed between the bright rays and Kathy's face that Mallory reacted. Shifting quickly, she moved her hand to provide the necessary shade. Unfortunately, it wasn't quick enough to cover Solly's protective action. Kathy had seen the black shadow move first and felt the shade.

"What was that?" she asked, lowering her voice to a whisper.

"Ummm, what was what?" Mallory replied.

"That!" Reaching up she pushed Mallory's hand away only to be assaulted by the sun again. Again, Mallory put her hand up and blocked the sun.

"That's the sunlight and stop moving so much. You may have injured your neck."

"My neck's fine and quit changing the subject. Something shaded my eyes before you did."

"Don't be ridiculous! There's no one here. You're suffering from a head injury so you must be imagining things."

Glancing slowly around, Kathy couldn't find anything to explain what she had seen.

"I...I guess you're right. I must be. God does my head hurt," Kathy groaned. Closing her eyes again, she relaxed against the headrest, enjoying the warm hand caressing her forehead and hair. Had she opened her eyes again, she would have seen Mallory using her cell phone to call for help. Neither hand was near her face.

That had been a long time ago. Although the two kept in touch for several years after college, they eventually lost contact with each other. The last Mallory had heard of Kathy, she had partnered up with a school teacher and moved to Memphis.

"You're awfully quiet," Mallory remarked, aware of her life-partner's withdrawal. It wasn't unusual for Solly to *disappear* somewhere within the deep recesses of her mind but it could be disconcerting at times. An indescribable loneliness would take over, leaving her feeling lost. Still, she understood the need for her *Les Gris* to have her own space, just as she needed to be alone at times.

I was searching for something, Solly said.

"And did you find it?" Mallory asked, curious.

Yes!

When Solly didn't say any more, Mallory knew the subject was closed. Even life-partners didn't share everything.

Once they arrived at the park, Mallory watched as Ridge made the rounds to several people sitting on the benches. Some knew him and called him by name. One elderly woman in particular slapped her knee joyfully, urging him to join her.

Ms. Joelson really loves him, you know. Ridge reminds her of Beebee.

"Beebee was a poodle for Christ's sake!" Mallory snorted. "Ridge isn't anything like her."

Physically no, but her Les Gris was similar to Ridge's. They shared a bond like us.

Stunned at the information, Mallory wasn't sure what to say.

"You mean they were friends?"

Is that how you would describe us? Solly asked, amused at the weak description. *They were more than friends. Are you surprised that animal Les Gris can share as intimate a bond as we do?"*

Mallory thought about the concept for a few moments and then realized that there was no reason for her not to accept it. Ridge was more than a companion to her so why couldn't animal Les Gris bond with each other the same way?

Humans are unique. Typically, they only bond with another human Les Gris. Animals, however, can actually bond outside of their species. That's why you'll see some strange mismatches once in awhile, like the lioness who kept adopting those small oryx in Kenya a few years ago. She had bonded with one as a cub.

191

"Damn! I thought it was just a freaky mental thing when I saw that documentary. I mean it can't be good for the species involved, especially if they're incompatible."

True! That was a sad misfortune. It was impossible for the lioness to protect the oryx from the other lions. For some species it works out fine. Cats and dogs, pigs and horses, those are pretty common actually. Even cats and birds seem to do okay. For the lioness and oryx, though, their worlds were too extreme. Maybe one day though.

"Maybe," Mallory agreed, watching Ridge as he nudged the old woman's palm with his nose. "He's always been a gentle soul."

He had a hard time for a while. Just like you. I think that's what makes your bond with him so strong.

Mallory smiled, remembering the first time she had seen him. Small and furry, he was a rambunctious pup who feared nothing. That was what impressed her the most. When the breeder brought him and his two littermates out for inspection and observation, Ridge wasted no time in pouncing on and chasing anything that caught his attention. Mallory soon became the main focal point of his fledgling attempts at herding and she realized that something about the young puppy felt... right.

That was five years ago. Since then, Ridge had proven his worth time and time again. Although gentle, he never hesitated to put himself in danger if it meant protecting Mallory. At first she was a little disconcerted by his protective displays but soon realized it seemed specific to the individual rather than all strangers. It was only after she reprimanded him once for growling at a young man walking toward them late one night that Solly decided to enlighten her about the reason.

He is warning him not to come closer, you know.

"Why? The boy looks harmless enough," Mallory replied.

Looks are deceiving. He's a predator and was going to attack you from behind once you passed him.

Mallory frowned.

"So why didn't you pick up on that? I thought *Les Gris* warned each other about things like this."

We try but he's irreparably flawed. They have been out of sync for so long they no longer function well. His Les Gris has withdrawn into the darkest recesses of this boy's mind and refuses to help him now.

"So how did Ridge know about him?"

Ridge's Les Gris sensed their dysfunction before I did. Animals are more sensitive to changes in people than humans. Perhaps their Les Gris share that quality. We know little about them but there's no reason to believe Ridge's life-partner isn't as intelligent as we are.

Mallory wasn't sure if she believed it or not but the explanation was as good as any. The important thing was that in protecting her from the potential assailant, he had forged an indestructible bond between them. He was no longer just a substitute companion for her own failed relationships, but a friend worthy of respect, love and most of all, equality.

I'm proud of you, Solly said, giving her a mental hug. *You're maturing.* Unsure how to respond, Mallory decided it was best not to ask what Solly meant. *Les Gris* could be very philosophical at times. Instead, she kneeled next to Ridge and gave him a big hug.

"Sorry about snapping at you like that, fella. I should have known you had a good reason for growling at him."

Ridge gave her a toothy grin and quick lick on the nose. All was forgiven.

* * *

Ridge continued nudging Mrs. Joelson's palm, enjoying the attention. She had a gentle touch, and he felt her loneliness.

193

Although Beebee was too old to play for long when he first met her in the park, she had still greeted the youngster with enthusiasm and pretended to get irritated at his youthful antics. For five years they continued playing their games, enjoying each other's company as only true friends could.

In the end, Ridge had sensed her failing health long before her human had and he comforted the old dog whenever they met at the park. On her last visit, he knew instinctively that he wouldn't see her again. Lying quietly next to her, he snuggled as close as possible in order to share his warmth.

Beebee had lost several pounds and shivered constantly from the cold even though she wore a thick knitted sweater. Between Ridge and the warm sun beating down upon them, the old dog felt warm and comforted. Relaxing, she had dozed for almost an hour enjoying her final moments with her young playmate.

Finally, Mrs. Joelson woke Beebee up so they could head home before it got too dark to see. Giving her a lick on her furry cheek, Ridge bid Beebee farewell. She stared unblinking at him for a few moments, her eyes clouded with cataracts, and then turned slowly to follow her human home, never looking back. They had said their farewells.

* * *

After making sure Mrs. Joelson was fine, Ridge dashed off to meet up with several other dogs for a game of *catch me if you can!* It was one of his favorite sports. Although he wasn't the fastest dog in the group, he was still able to tag most of the competition through agility and determination. His herding skills gave him an advantage over the other dogs running around. Still, for some reason, smaller or older dogs occasionally managed to *tag* him because of a clumsy fall or unexplainable mistake.

Watching his antics, Mallory shook her head.

"I think he does that on purpose. The only time he seems that clumsy or absent-minded is here," she commented.

He knows some of them don't stand a chance. It builds their confidence and inspires them. It's important for dogs to be confident. They're more stable.

"I suppose!"

For almost an hour Ridge romped with his playmates. Occasionally he would break away to investigate the new arrivals or check back with Mrs. Joelson.

Normally, he refused to take food from anyone but Mallory or his caretakers at the vet, but he always made an exception for the elderly woman when she shared her sandwiches. Gently he would take the offered portions and slowly chew them, savoring every bite.

This time when they were finished, he took the empty paper lunch bag from her hand as usual and carried it to the nearest trashcan. Then with a happy yelp, he bounded off to join the rest of the dogs.

Now that is a class act, Solly commented. *Some people could take lessons from him.*

"Yeah, he really is special. He learned that on his own. I don't know what I'd do if anything ever happened to him."

As Ridge began herding some of the smaller dogs into a tight circle, a large lab puppy came running up and bounced around him enthusiastically. Distracted, Ridge never saw a small Chihuahua/Poodle mixed breed sneak up and nip him playfully. The little dog had known Ridge for years and knew he wasn't in any danger of being harmed. Ridge was always gentle with smaller dogs but loved to rough-house with the larger, more exuberant ones.

Deciding she needed to head home, Mallory was about to call to Ridge when Solly interrupted her.

The owner of the puppy is unstable.

"Unstable how?" Mallory asked, glancing at the young man sitting on a nearby bench. She had noticed him entering the park dragging the puppy on the leash, but thought the dog was just shy. Now, after noticing the youth's hunched shoulders and vacant expression, she knew something was wrong.

He abuses the puppy. Lumien, his Les Gris, can't communicate with him or control him. He says his life-partner is a sociopath and is planning to kill the dog as an experiment. This will be the fifth one this year.

Mallory was horrified. Watching Ridge and the pup chasing each other, she would never have guessed the animal was being mistreated.

Ridge's life-partner stabilizes her while they're together. He had hoped to buy her time until she could escape, but it may be too late. She's damaged, but that can be corrected. It's what the boy is planning that worries me. I think he intends on carrying out his plans in the next few days.

"So we need to get her away from her owner quickly. Can you get this bastard's *Les Gris* to help?"

Lumien is willing to do anything to save the puppy. He feels guilty because he couldn't save the others. This is his chance to redeem himself.

"Surely Lumien isn't blaming himself. There's only so much a *Les Gris* can do to assist its life-partner," Mallory reasoned.

True, but Les Gris don't accept failure well, especially when it creates suffering for the innocent. All animals deserve respect and compassion.

Mallory gave an unconscious nod.

"How can we help them? Is there a way to help the boy? I can call Belle. Maybe the Society can do something."

No! It's too late to help him. It's only a matter of time before he does something more horrible than what he's already done. Lumien wants to end this before that happens.

"Surely there's some..."

There's nothing. Lumien doesn't make this decision lightly. It's against everything we believe in to destroy our life-partner. He'll be lost forever.

Mallory felt helpless. For a *Les Gris* to become lost was the ultimate horror. Shaking her head, she wished she could think of something, but she trusted Solly's judgment.

"How are we going to rescue the puppy? It's not like we can just walk over and take him...and then what? You know we can't bring him to the apartment. Only one pet per unit, remember? He's going to need a good home."

For several minutes Mallory and Solly searched their minds, trying to decide how they could resolve this. In the end, it was Ridge that solved the problem for them. Teasing the puppy with his antics, he enticed him further and further away from his human until they were within a few feet of Mrs. Joelson. Then, nudging the puppy toward her, he backed away, sat down and watched. Occasionally, Ridge would look at the puppy's human to make sure he was still sitting on the bench.

* * *

Leaning forward, Mrs. Joelson peered intently at the black bundle of fur crouched nervously in front of her.

"Why Ridge, what have we here?" Mrs. Joelson asked, reaching out to pet the young dog. When he backed away, Ridge moved forward and bumped the youngster with his nose, forcing him closer again. "No, no, Ridge. He's frightened, poor little fellow."

Leaning down, she examined the puppy and frowned. "Oh my! Someone hasn't been very nice to you! Look how tight that collar is. We need to do something about that before it strangles you. Can you bring him a little closer, Ridge? These old hands don't work as well as they used to."

Immediately Ridge shouldered the puppy again. Giving the bigger dog a baleful look he inched toward the woman and hunkered down in front of her feet. When the hand reached for his collar, he growled and then whined.

"Now, now, don't be afraid. I won't hurt you."

Closing his eyes, he waited for the pain that always followed human contact. Instead, after a few short tugs on his collar, he felt the tightness disappear. Then the hand stroked his head a few times. The touch was gentle, unlike his owner's.

"Now, doesn't that feel better?" the human asked. Wagging his tail slightly, he showed his agreement. Suddenly, both were startled by a harsh voice yelling at them.

"Hey lady, what the fuck are you doing to my dog?" the boy called out, marching toward them angrily. Stopping next to the puppy, he grabbed the frightened animal by its neck and started to pick him up.

"Young man, that's no way to treat an animal," Mrs. Joelson chastised, shaking her finger at him.

"Mind your own damn business, lady," the boy snarled. "Unless you want..." Before he could finish his threat, he heard a low throaty growl. Glancing around he saw Ridge a few feet away glaring at him, lips curled upward exposing large canine teeth. Unwisely, he released the puppy and swung at the angry dog, only to find himself flat on his back seconds later with his face inches away from the dog's mouth.

The look in the animal's eyes left him no doubt about what would happen if he moved even slightly. Footsteps caught his attention but he was afraid to even turn his head. Hopefully, it was someone coming to his aid. Then he'd take care of the old woman and her damned dog even if he had to follow them home.

"Well, well," Mallory snapped angrily, stopping with her feet only inches from the boy's head. "I think we've solved one problem quite nicely. Now, asshole, what was that you were saying?" she demanded, nudging the boy's head with her right foot.

"Umm, could you get that damn dog off me?" he asked, still unable to take his eyes off the fangs inches from his face. *I'll get you too, bitch,* he thought but wisely kept the threat to himself.

"Sure. After you apologize, of course."

At first it looked as if the boy was going to object but another growl from Ridge convinced him otherwise.

"Uh, sure. Okay, I'm sorry lady. I mean...I was just mouthing off. I wasn't going to do anything."

He's lying. He's going to follow Mrs. Joelson home once he leaves, said Solly.

Then we'll just give her an escort. Is there anything Lumien can do to help us?

Lumien says he'll take care of everything. He wants us to take the puppy.

"Not a bad idea." Turning to the elderly woman, Mallory helped her to her feet. "Mrs. Joelson, I need to ask you a favor. Could you puppy-sit this little guy for a few days, at least? I don't think it's wise to send him home with this guy."

Mrs. Joelson hesitated. It had only been a few months since Beebee had died. She wasn't sure she was ready for another dog.

"I'd really appreciate it, Mrs. Joelson. It's that or letting this creep have him back."

"Well, I guess it'll be fine for a few days. Mind you, though, I'm not saying I'm going to keep him longer. It wouldn't be right with Beebee being gone for such a short while."

"I don't think Beebee would mind. She'd want you to have company."

When the boy started to object, Mallory turned her icy gaze on him, daring him to say anything. Something in her eyes sent a chill down his spine. Swallowing, he inhaled deeply trying to stem a sudden unfamiliar fear. For the first time in his life, he was the prey, not the predator. It was a feeling he didn't like.

To make matters worse, the dog had moved his muzzle even closer to the boy's face. Several drops of drool slipped from the lower jaw into his mouth. The urge to gag was strong but the expression in the dog's eyes left him even more terrified.

You know Ridge is doing that intentionally don't you? He's enjoying showing off for all of us.

I figured that out, Mallory said.

Unaware of the exchange, Mrs. Joelson patted Mallory's arm affectionately.

"We'd better be getting home then. I'll need to pick up a few things at the store. I need some type of leash too. I don't want to use that one," she said, pointing to the large chain-link one the young boy had been holding. "It's way too heavy for such a little fellow."

"No problem. Take Ridge's. He doesn't need one." Mallory reached into her coat pocket. Snapping the leash onto the puppy's collar, she handed the end to Mrs. Joelson and then gave her a hug. "This little fellow is going to need a lot of love. He hasn't been treated very well."

"I have plenty of that," Mrs. Joelson assured her, not realizing she had already made her commitment to keep him. "Come on, little fella. Let's go home." Gently tugging on the leash, Mrs. Joelson moved slowly toward the park exit. At seventy-one, she suffered from arthritis, making walking a little painful. Still, she was in good health and had several good years left in her. Mallory had no doubt the two would share a rich and rewarding life together.

Turning to the boy still on the ground, Mallory motioned for Ridge to let him up.

"Beat it," she said, "and don't come back."

Without saying a word the young man stood and started to walk away. Before he could take two steps though, Mallory's hand shot out and grabbed his arm, spinning him around.

"I suggest you leave the way you came," she advised, motioning toward a busy intersection in the opposite direction of Mrs. Joelson's departure.

Hands in his pockets and head bowed, he mumbled something foul under his breath, but never even glanced at Mallory, Ridge or the old woman as she disappeared around a corner. Already his mind was on ways to vent his frustration and anger over the humiliation he had experienced. He was also pissed off at having to find something else for his experiment.

"What do you think he's going to do now?" Mallory asked, watching him until he was almost at the intersection.

Lumien says he's thinking of grabbing his neighbor's dog but I wouldn't worry too much about it, Solly replied.

"I think —"

Before she could finish her thought, she heard brakes squealing and jerked her head around to see what had happened. A crowd had gathered around someone lying on the street in front of a bus.

Lumien took care of everything. My people will honor him.

Mallory felt Solly's sadness and wished they could have done more.

It's enough that we saved the puppy. It's what Lumien wanted and cause for celebration. Let's go play with Ridge. He is the hero of the day.

Smiling, Mallory knelt down and wrapped her arms around her dog. Giving her a toothy grin, Ridge licked her face a few times and then wriggled away and dashed off. Mallory knew the game... *catch me if you can.* Laughing she shook her head.

"That's it? That's all the appreciation I get for helping him?"

You really didn't expect something dramatic did you?

"Actually, yes."

Standing, Mallory ran toward Ridge, arms spread wide as if attempting to grab him. Watching his mistress's antics, he gave a happy woof and loped toward her. It was a good day.

The End

About the Author

FRAN HECKROTTE lives in sunny South Carolina with her husband. She spent three years in Alaska enjoying hiking, camping, gold panning and working part time at a local ranch. After moving to the South she became a police officer for five years, then left law enforcement to become a carpenter. Now she owns a property management company. As time permits, she likes to travel to Montreal, Canada to ski and do some hiking.

About the Copy Editor

Cindy Burke has had a lifelong interest in journalism and fiction writing. She started as a newsroom assistant and has contributed several articles to local newspapers. Her science fiction book, "Intimate Space: A Feminist Utopian Romp Through the Galaxy," was published in 2015.

Burke was born in Savannah, GA and lived for several years in California, Georgia and Florida before moving to Upstate South Carolina in 1998. She is a social justice advocate and Vice President of the Clemson Alumni Society for Equality (CASE), an alumni group that has established two student scholarships.

Her family is spread across the Southeast, including two sons, a sous chef and a navy technician. She lives with her husband, a computer analyst and fellow sci-fi and fantasy buff. Burke writes from their home located in the foothills of the beautiful Blue Ridge Mountains. You can reach her at www.cindyburke.com.

About the Cover Artist

Patty G. Henderson is an author, publisher and artist and all around bohemian at heart. An independent author, she launched her own publishing imprint, Blanca Rosa Publishing. She writes Gothic Historical Romances and has published four so far, THE SECRET OF LIGHTHOUSE POINTE, CASTLE OF DARK SHADOWS, PASSION FOR VENGEANCE, and SHADOWS OF THE HEART. She has also penned four Brenda Strange Supernatural Mysteries, Comfortable wearing several creative hats, Patty is an accomplished artist as well as author. She's done popular book cover artwork for many mainstream mystery and horror authors and lesbian authors via her graphic arts business, Boulevard Photografica, in addition to a nearly complete immersion in indie writing and publishing. You can reach Patty via her author web site: www.pattyghenderson.com or check out her graphics and book cover professional web site: www.boulevardphotografica.yolasite.com.

About the Formatter

eB Format does ebook conversions from any file format to MOBI(KF8), ePub, Smashwords Style Guide specifications, and CreateSpace formats. We're your go-to team for professional service on a personal level at affordable prices. Request a quote at www.ebformat.com today.

Other Titles by Fran Heckrotte

The Illusionist (First in The Illusionist Series)

DAKOTA DEVEREAUX, an investigative journalist, is on a mission to uncover the secrets of Yemaya, the Illusionist. However, in her quest for an exposé on this mysterious woman, she uncovers more than she bargained for. Dakota is targeted by a power hungry CEO determined to learn the Illusionist's secret at all costs, and a madman intent on fulfilling his perverted fantasies.

From Moldova, land of the legendary werewolf, to the Transylvania and the Carpathian Mountains, two souls must battle the dark forces of evil for their lives and their love.

Bloodlust (Second in The Illusionist Series)

YEMAYA AND DAKOTA have just returned to the Illusionist's homeland for a well-earned vacation when they are informed that several villagers have been savagely attacked and killed by something or someone. At the same time, a young Carpi woman is found lying unconscious near the outskirts of Teraclia. Comatose, she is unable to tell anyone what has happened and science can provide no answers. Two small wounds on her throat raise the old specter of the vampire, a legend the locals of the Transylvanian community are very familiar with and still believe to this day.

The Illusionist and her partner search for the truth behind these attacks. Will they fall prey to the murderous bloodlust that surrounds them, or will they succeed in stopping this heinous reign of terror?

Lilith (Third in The Illusionist Series)

YEMAYA, the Illusionist, and her journalist partner, Dakota, find themselves embroiled in a search for the person responsible for the rape and torture of a young Carpi woman attending a university in the States. When they decide to visit a local nightclub for "women only," they find the owner and her employees unusual. Dakota feels mysteriously attracted to one of the clientele while Yemaya recognizes a kindred spirit in Lilith, the club's owner. Spiritual ancestors, missing whores, a sadistic exporter and new acquaintances lead the two lovers into an adventure of Biblical proportions.

Lilith! She was a demoness, as old as humanity itself. Now she is the owner of a "women's only" nightclub and part owner of the Sisterhood, a small group of whores who have banded together to create a better life for themselves. It is her job to protect the women who are putting so much trust in her. When a local pimp decides to eliminate his competition, Lilith and her two demon partners want revenge and no one knows better how to exact it than demons. This is a revelation of the past, the present and the events that forever changed the course of human history.

Les Gris, The Shadow People (Fourth in The Illusionist Series)

THEY ARE LES GRIS, the Shadow People, and are as much a part of us as we are them. As children, we talked to them, played with them and disclosed our innermost fears, secrets and dreams. They patiently listened, comforted and encouraged us. Over time, though, we outgrew our *imaginary* friends and forgot them. For those few who didn't, mankind's very existence will be determined by the strength of the bond between a small group of humans and their life-partners, *Les Gris.*

Saira (Fifth in The Illusionist Series)

SAIRA WAS A TRAVELER. Even her name meant 'traveler'. Her entire existence was dedicated to making the journey to seek answers to the questions that plagued her. Sometimes she felt as if she were a pawn in a game she didn't understand but knew her destiny was hers to decide. She chose to let the uncertainty of time make the decisions for her.

In Saira, her curiosity not only gets her into trouble but creates a series of events that affects not only the mortal world but the spirit world too. Yemaya, Dakota, Mari and Maopa will find their lives turned topsy-turvy and Saira will learn an emotion she had never experienced before...fear.

Warrior Demoness (Sixth in The Illusionist Series)

SHE WAS SABNOCK, a demon, who, like the Phoenix, lived and died many times because she chose to live amongst mortals rather than spend eternity babysitting the legions of the Underlord. There were no longer battles to be fought in the Underworld so the ex-commander left her realm to live with the humans as a human. Falling in love, she now had to choose between her vow to live and die as a mortal or live and love as a demon, not knowing if her lover could accept the truth. The wrong decision would condemn her to a life of loneliness — and for a demon, life was eternity.

Solaria (Futuristic Science Fiction)

THE FIRST AWARENESS of existence was a chaotic flash of colors, meaningless and yet in an odd way logical. Why, she isn't sure. Birth is the most significant event in life, and yet it is never memorable, at least not for the newborn. But then, she really isn't a newborn, even though it is the first day of her life. She is 1A526, the first of her kind, an artificially intelligent blend of technology and bio-mechanics. Created to serve humans, Solaria and her AI programmer, Carley, soon discover the company funding the Hubot Project has more sinister motives. If Solaria is to fulfill the hopes of the woman who gave her existence meaning, she has to become the human her programmer dreamed of and take down Future Dynamicon, the company that created her.

Future Perfect (Sequel to Solaria)

PRIMERIS WAS a Hubot, designed to serve humans. Her existence depended on her ability to complete her assignments...which she always did with a cold, emotionless detachment. Now, her perfect record was going to be tested to its limits. In her attempts to find and capture Solaria, another Hubot, Primeris is forced to either disobey her directive of obedience or become the human she never wanted to be.

The Order of the Healers was exactly that, healers. Their mission was to move humanity forward, even if it meant saving the worst of mankind. Chantelle is a Singer, a member of a small sub-group of Healers, whose latest calling takes her on a mission that will test her gift to its limit, and leave her wondering if her success will lead to humanity's downfall.

Rapture, Sins of the Sinners
By A.C. Henley and Fran Heckrotte

THERE'S A SERIAL killer running rampant in the state of Texas and she's not yet quenched her thirst for blood. Practiced in her craft, she is good with a blade and leaves no trace behind.

When a pattern becomes evident in murders in Ft. Worth, savvy detective Agnes Kelly-Elliott is assigned to the case. With her partner Jeff, Agnes quickly starts to work to solve the murders happening in her district.

From all across the state and with no apparent end in sight, Texas Ranger Cochetta Lovejoy is certain she knows just who this killer might be. She relentlessly pursues her suspect when she meets up with her, and sets in motion events which can never be undone.

Odyssey of the Butterfly

TAKE A JOURNEYthrough space, time and the imagination...all with a common thread, butterflies. If you like science fiction, fantasy, zombies or romance, these five short stories offer a little of each, and more. Can you solve the mystery of the butterfly or will it leave you wondering the next time you see one flitting by?

www.ingramcontent.com/pod-product-compliance
Lightning Source LLC
Chambersburg PA
CBHW051504170626
46811CB00002B/643

* 9 7 8 1 9 3 9 9 5 0 2 1 5 *